ALIEN
IN A
BOTTLE

ALSO BY
Kathy MackeL

CAN OF WORMS

EGGS IN ONE BASKET

FROM THE HORSE'S MOUTH

Kathy
MackeL

ALIEN
IN A
BOTTLE

🎬 HARPERCOLLINS*PUBLISHERS*

Library of Congress Cataloging-in-Publication Data

Mackel, Kathy. Alien in a bottle / Kathy Mackel.— 1st ed.   p. cm.

Summary: With the help of a star-gazing classmate and an unusual assortment of
aliens from outer space, teenager Sean Winger tries to find a way to convince his
parents to let him pursue his dream of becoming a glassblower.

ISBN 0-06-029281-4 — ISBN 0-06-029282-2 (lib. bdg.)

[1. Extraterrestrial beings—Fiction. 2. Glassblowing and working
—Fiction.] I. Title.

PZ7.M1955Al 2004 [Fic]—dc21   2003004443

Typography by Karin Paprocki

1 2 3 4 5 6 7 8 9 10

❖ First Edition

To Katie and Jenny,
who make dreams rise

Many thanks to master glassblower
PETER GREENWOOD
(www.petergreenwood.com),
who opened his studio to me and delighted me
with the craft of glassblowing and his skill.

Thanks also to
DAVID WENTZELL
for his help and direction.
And always, my husband, Steve,
for his patience and support.

Author's Note

Glassblowing is an amazing and elegant craft. It is no exaggeration to say that a glassblower's furnace is as hot as the surface of the Sun—which makes glassblowing a dangerous art to master. DO NOT TRY MELTING OR SHAPING GLASS ON YOUR OWN. If you are interested in working with glass, contact your local arts center, university, or glassblowers' association for information on student classes.

Oh yes, and don't bring any aliens, genies, or strangers home, either.

ALIEN
IN A
BOTTLE

1

It was the perfect way for Sean Winger to end a putrid day—up to his eyebrows in soiled diapers, rotting pizza, and soggy newspapers. The way his life had been trashed, it only made sense to complete the picture with a Dumpster dive at Crane's Neck Beach. The way Sean saw it, he was simply fulfilling his destiny.

Little did he know he was about to discover it.

The putrid day had begun at breakfast. Sean's parents, Geoff and Dorothy Winger, chewed their high-fiber cereal while they digested their high-minded *Financial Times*.

"Uh-hum," Sean croaked, trying to clear the willies from his throat. "I have an announcement to make."

His parents peered over their reading glasses: gold-rimmed for Mom and tortoiseshell for Dad.

"You know how I have to choose which high school to go to?" Sean began. The eighth graders had just finished a tour of Squannacook's four secondary schools. They had to register for one by the end of March.

His father narrowed his eyes. "And which have you chosen?"

Sean deepened his voice, trying to sound mature. "I've decided not to go to any of them. They aren't"—he paused, trying to remember the impressive words he had looked up last night—"*relevant* to my career aspirations."

"And what exactly is irrelevant about the four schools you have to choose from?" his father asked. "The four schools that we support with our hard-earned tax dollars?"

"They stink!" Sean blurted. So much for being mature, but his whole life was at stake here. He would be miserable at any of the district's high schools.

The high school was a repeat of middle school—lockers slamming, girls jabbering, jocks strutting, teachers nagging. The tech school was a hornet's nest—kids rushing from class to shop to jobs, buzzing like wasps around roadkill.

The charter school was a sham—wannabe artists, pseudophilosophers, and hack writers, all moaning how no one appreciated them. The exam school was out— Sean knew his place, and it wasn't at the head of the class.

There was only one place where Sean could be truly happy. "I applied to Monadnock Museum School," he said.

"Wonderful." Dad moaned. "Let's start the day right by ruining breakfast."

Mom shushed him with a wave of her spoon. "What makes you think the museum school is a better fit for you?"

"They have all the usual academic subjects, plus sculpture, painting, woodworking, and other stuff," Sean said.

"What other stuff?" His father took off his spectacles, as if he could stare some sense into his son without glass in the way. But that was the thing—*glass* of one sort or another always got between Sean and his father.

Sean launched into speed-speak, hoping his father would miss the one detail that would make his blood pressure go ballistic. "Stone carving, watercolors, pottery, silk-screening, glassblowing, performance art, and other cool things too numerous to mention."

"No. You are not going there." His father bit each word like it was a tough piece of liver he couldn't wait to spit out. "And you are not doing that."

That? He wouldn't even say the word *glassblowing*.

"Why not?" Sean asked, as if he hadn't heard *why not* a thousand times.

"Sean, you're so handy and talented," his mother said. "Glassblowing will probably be just one of many hobbies you enjoy when you grow up."

"Hobby? Glassblowing is more than a hobby! Why can't you see that it's my life?" Sean cried.

"Because artists starve. Your friend Franklin Zarkoff was a perfect example of that," his father said.

"And as much as we enjoy your creativity," his mother added, "we strongly feel that starving isn't in your best interest."

Sean lowered his head into his hands. Couldn't they see that he was starving now? That if he couldn't be a glassblower he would crumble like a piece of bran toast and just blow away?

That afternoon outstunk the morning like a month-old tuna sandwich outstinks a gym locker.

Three days a week, after school, Sean went to the Exploring the Arts Program. While other kids hung out at the mall or played basketball, he and his fellow artists created great art.

On that afternoon, Susan Long worked in acrylics, dabbing a baby-blue sky with hot-pink clouds. A sunflower sun with a happy face rose over the lime-green trees. Luke Chang molded chaws of bubblegum into an edifice called the *Notre Gum Cathedral*. His stained-glass windows glittered with grape, and his soldiers sported strawberry hunchbacks.

Jenna painted rocks to look like plantar warts. Paul made papier-mâché canaries from the telephone book. Leah crafted the *Titanic* from soda cans and dental floss.

Sean was the true artist of the group—an honest-togoodness glassblower. At least, he would be, if someone would let him actually blow glass.

"Too dangerous," Ms. Flack had said when he applied to the EAP. She allowed Sean to do lampwork—the shaping of beads and other small items over a small open flame. It was like asking Leonardo da Vinci to paint with a floor mop, but it was better than nothing.

That afternoon Sean set up to make turquoise beads with silver swirls. While blue-green glass pellets melted in a ceramic basin, he snipped strips of aluminum foil to twist through the beads. When everything was ready, he dipped his blowpipe into the glass.

"Ms. Flack," Luke called out, "you've got company." Mr. Vincent, the middle school's assistant principal, waved from the door.

"I'll be right back," Ms. Flack said, and stepped out into the hall.

Susan glanced at her watch. "Ten minutes."

"Minimum," Luke said with a laugh. Everyone knew Ms. Flack looked forward to her afternoon coffee with Mr. Vincent.

Sean rotated the pipe, keeping the glass fluid. Ten minutes without adult supervision. What harm could one little puff do?

Too dangerous, Ms. Flack's voice nagged in his head.

How can I be a glassblower if I'm not allowed to blow glass?

5

You promised, Ms. Flack reminded him.

You'll starve, his father warned.

Starving isn't good for a growing boy, his mother added.

All of you, just shut up! Sean put the blowpipe to his mouth and puffed.

As the clump bubbled, the nagging voices in Sean's head were swept away by Franklin Zarkoff's coaxing. *Turn the glass over the flame; keep it fluid.* Just like the old days in the Zarkoff Studio. *That's it, son. Keep the temperature even so the glass doesn't crack.* The master artist, passing on his craft to a young apprentice. *Just blow, steady and light.*

A perfect blue-green sphere formed. Sean had a sudden vision of a rich green world under a sparkling blue sky. It would take two blowpipes; nesting glass within glass was an advanced technique. He could do it, he knew he could!

Why not add a third layer of glass to form crystal clouds? The Winger Technique, they would call it. Artists all over the world would beg for his secret. Sean wouldn't share it with anyone—except for maybe his apprentice, if he ever had one.

Sean Winger was still dreaming of glory when he heard the *crack.*

The glass bubble had grown to the size of a melon. The underside of the globe, held over the open flame, glowed orange while the top had cooled to ruby.

Crack. The sound every glassblower fears, the sound of glass about to—

POP!

Ms. Flack came back in just in time to see Sean's world shatter into a hundred pieces. She didn't say a word; she just frowned and pointed at the door, like the Grim Reaper sending Sean to his doom.

If Sean had known that day would end in a Dumpster, he would have pulled the covers over his head and slept until his eighteenth birthday. But instead, he biked to Crane's Neck Beach after supper.

He had a study date with Olivia Ricci, the smartest kid in school. Their assignment was to chart the constellations as they appeared an hour after sunset. The beach had been Olivia's idea. "Because it's far away from the lights of stores and traffic," she had said.

Sean got why she wanted the beach. He just didn't get why Olivia wanted him. She was so precise; her numbers always added up and her lines were always straight.

Sean preferred swirling colors, streaming lights, and shifting borders. In the real world, nothing added up perfectly. It was up to the artist to find the beauty in the chaos.

Olivia was already at Crane's Neck when Sean arrived.

She was so focused on her telescope, she didn't even say hi. Sean shivered and zipped up his jacket. He wasn't insulted that Olivia hadn't noticed him. She didn't even seem to notice the harsh wind coming off the water or the salt-stained ice at the shoreline.

A cold March night at the ocean wasn't Sean's idea of fun. But he needed to be here—flunking science would be worse than numb toes or sand in his shoes. "Hi," he said.

"Oh. You're here," she said. She didn't take her eye from the telescope; she just handed Sean a pad of graph paper and motioned him to the blanket. "You do the western half of the sky and I'll chart the eastern half."

Sean was done in a quick ten minutes. Sketching was like breathing to him.

"Wow," Olivia said when he showed her his work. "It's almost perfect."

"Almost?"

"Well, you made whitecaps on the ocean. They're visually attractive but proportionately incorrect. And the horizon should just be a straight line."

"Whatever." Sean erased the life out of the ocean and redrew it as a dull line. Then he glanced up at Olivia to find out what he was supposed to do next.

Maybe it was the way Olivia's hair had come loose in the wind. Gold and curly, it shimmered around her face like a candle flame. Maybe it was the way she stared at the sky, as if she could will it to spill its secrets. Maybe it was her eyes, so brown that they captured everything they saw.

This was not the Olivia Ricci who pulled her hair tight from her face and wore sensible shoes and raised her hand before the teacher even asked a question. This was an Olivia Ricci who took Sean's breath away.

He could see the glass rising from the fire. Clean lines for intelligence, deep curves for mystery. *Olivia Rising*, he would call the work. He would never sell it; he would give it to Olivia to remind her of this night, this time—

"Hey! Earth to Winger! You're off in La-La Land," Olivia said.

"Oh. That's kind of where I live," Sean said. "Sorry."

"That's okay. I live there sometimes too."

Then why have we never met there? Sean wanted to ask. But words wouldn't come. For a long time, the only sound came from the waves slapping the shore.

Olivia finally spoke. "I come here every night to watch the stars."

"Why?" he asked. "It's not like the stars change much from yesterday to today. Or from billion years to trillion years."

Olivia sat next to him. "Can I trust you, Winger?"

She smelled like cinnamon. Sean felt a good kind of dizzy, the kind you get from being on a merry-go-round. "Sure," he mumbled.

Olivia looked around as if to make sure no one else was listening. Then she put her mouth near his ear and whispered, "The stars are only part of what I'm watching for."

Sean's heart banged so loud he couldn't think. "Like storm clouds? Or spy planes?"

"Never mind. It's not important." Olivia got up and fiddled with her telescope.

"Yes, it is. So tell me," he said, standing next to her.

They looked out over the ocean. The border between sky and sea was lost in darkness. The air was crisp, salty. Away from streetlights and cars, the world seemed endless.

"I said you can trust me," Sean said. He kept looking over the water. If he looked at Olivia, she might pull away again.

He heard her take a deep breath. Then she began in a hushed voice, totally unlike her I-know-every-answer way of speaking. "The sky is infinite," she said. "And you can't even count the stars. So the possibilities of what's out there are endless. So endless that they become probabilities."

"And?"

"It becomes *probable* that someone from out there will come here to visit us. And I don't want to miss that."

"You mean—visitors from outer space?"

Olivia slowly nodded, still not meeting his eyes.

Sean could see it all as if it were unfolding right there, in front of them—Crane's Neck overrun with tourists from the stars.

Bigheaded aliens slopped on sunscreen. Octopus-limbed extraterrestrials bounced beach balls. Green-faced imps body-surfed. Lizard-skinned crawlers peeled off flakes of sunburn. "We're here!" they cried in voices that twanged like banjos.

Sean began to laugh. He laughed hard, he laughed long.

Even when Olivia slammed her telescope into its case, Sean kept laughing. He gulped air, bit his tongue, pinched himself. But he just couldn't stop laughing.

Until he realized that Olivia was gone. Then he wanted to cry.

Instead, Sean Winger did the next best thing. He headed for the Dumpster.

2

Dinn Tauro would rather die than dream.

Dinn and his crew of space jockeys had conquered the slime-spewing goliaths of Sputz. They had explored the rock-heaving plains of Gnarl. They had navigated through the brown holes of Undoo.

Dinn Tauro had laughed in the face of peril and spit in the face of danger. He feared nothing—until that scum-kissing, rot-licking baggage, Tagg Orion, sold him the Dream Ring. Now Dinn Tauro feared sleep more than death itself.

Dinn had tried for eighteen standard Solars to stay awake. But he couldn't resist sleep any more than he could resist gravity. With his crew standing guard, Dinn laid down his weary head. If only he could sleep and not dream. . . .

Dinn's throne was forty feet high, sparkling with precious stones the size of nobfruits. His subjects covered the kingdom from horizon to horizon, shouting his praises.

A regal cat curled in Dinn's lap. He stopped waving so he

could pet the creature. Its coat was silky, its ears were velvety, its teeth were—

—impaled in Dinn's hand! The creature's yellow fangs tore through Dinn's skin like a gargolyte tears through its prey. But this was no gargolyte. This was a gutter rat!

Dinn howled with rage. The creature leaped off his lap and flew into the clouds.

The crowd cheered. Shaking off his pain, Dinn stood, acknowledging their admiration. The cheers died. Dinn waved his arms, motioning to the crowd to continue. When Dinn heard the first giggle, he thought perhaps his subjects were shy.

When the giggle rolled into chuckles, he thought they were silly. When the chuckles burst into laughter and the laughter avalanched into guffaws, Dinn reached for his head-whacker. But his scabbard was gone, along with every stitch of his clothing.

Dinn Tauro stood on a throne, forty feet high, naked for his whole world to see!

The crowd took up a chant. "The king has no clothes! Long live the king . . . just not where we have to look at him!"

Dinn scrambled for a hiding place. There, under the throne—a locker, used for storing official proclamations. But he couldn't remember the combination! He spun and whirled and crunched his brain, but the numbers wouldn't come.

And now his fingers weren't working right. Dinn looked at his hands—there were stumps where his fingers had been!

His fingers were gone but now the gutter rat was back. It swished its tail as if it were enjoying a joke. Some joke—the creature's yellow teeth dripped with Dinn's fingers!

"Someone wake me up from this dream!" Dinn screamed.

"Why bother?" said the rat. "There's only more where this one came from."

"Wake up, Your Loftiness!"

Laser fire zinged around Dinn Tauro's head. While he had slept, a battle had raged. Dinn strapped on his head-whacker. He checked to make sure he was wearing pants, and then he raced down the corridor. A gutter rat the size of a boulder-roller held the ship's bridge under siege.

When Dinn Tauro's dreams came *to life*, they became larger *than life*.

"Your Loftiness!" The Navigator gasped. "Stay back—this is the worst creature your dreams have spawned yet."

"It drinks in laser fire like draco sap," the Sergeant-at-Arms cried.

Dinn Tauro sheathed his head-whacker. "Put away your gut-burners! I know what the foul thing wants."

As his crew gasped in disbelief, Dinn scratched behind the rat's ear. The monster was so huge that Dinn could fit his head in one of its hairy nostrils. Its eyes slowly closed. Its head slumped to the floor. Within seconds, the beast snored like a trash masher.

"What is your pleasure, Loftiness?" his Waste Officer

asked. "Shall I jettison it to the seventh dimension and let it twist in the currents? Or drop it into here-and-now space, where the vacuum will suck out its guts?"

"No," Dinn said. "I want it kept alive."

"But why, Loftiness?" the Waste Officer asked. He had been looking forward to splattering guts.

"But why, Loftiness?" the Sergeant-at-Arms asked. She knew that they must strike while they were able. One day, Dinn Tauro would dream up a monster too horrible to contain.

"Because when I find that scum-swilling, skunk-spawning Tagg Orion, I will feed him to this filthy rat!" His crew gasped. When Dinn Tauro made a promise, he kept it, even if he had to explode red stars and blow up black holes to make it happen.

"If I have to go to the end of the endless galaxies and back," Dinn Tauro swore, "I will find Tagg Orion and make him pay!"

Tagg Orion had been to the end of the galaxy and back, but Shuala was still his favorite flea market. Jeebers wheeled in from every star system in the Amalgamated Planets—jeebers with galactic credits to spend if you had something to sell.

Tagg Orion could sell the skin of a snake. Of course, the

snake could turn around and bite you, which was why Tagg never stayed long enough to handle customer returns.

An Aquarian niblet sniffed at the toy table. Tagg pulled a game out of the pile. "Ever play Candyworld?"

"That's a baby game," the niblet snarled. But his eyestalks bounced with curiosity.

"This isn't a baby game," Tagg said. "In fact, maybe I'd better ask for some proof of age before I let you handle it."

The nib's stalks twisted. Aquarians do not like to be hustled, even ones barely out of their shells. "Fiddlespits!"

"You don't believe me?" Tagg handed the niblet a set of spinners. "Throw 'em."

The spinners tumbled to the board, each showing one black spot. "Scatt's eyes!" Tagg boomed. "Move two spaces."

The niblet pushed the game piece to a glowing pink space. The game piece vibrated. The space on the board dimpled, then mushroomed outward. Lollibams erupted from the game board!

The nib's stalks spun so hard, his eyes bugged out. Tagg mentally increased the price of the game. "So, what do you think?"

"I can get lollibams anywhere." The niblet slurped a bammer bigger than his head.

Barely out of his husk and the kid already knew how to bargain! Tagg was impressed. "But can you get khokolatt where you come from?"

"What is this khokolatt? Some kind of medicine, like that scumslice my mahm makes me take when my nose lobes get gassy?"

Tagg lowered his voice. "Khokolatt is undiscovered in this part of the galaxy. You could be the first to get a taste . . . " Tagg picked up the spinners.

"Let me roll again!"

"It could be yours. The lollibams, the gumblocks, the snutcrunches. And the mysterious, astounding khokolatt. When you buy the game."

"Mahm!" the niblet hollered.

A puffy Aquarian mahm fluttered over, her finagles laden with curtain rods and canning jars. "Did you find something you want, Arnolt?"

The nib nodded.

"How much?" the mahm asked.

"Well, I was asking forty G.C.s." Tagg kept his smile modest. No use wasting wattage on a close-pocketed Aquarian.

"Ridiculous!" she snapped. "Forty galactic credits is too much for a secondhand game."

"It's in flawless condition. And I do have to at least cover my costs. But seeing that your son has his heart set on it, I could let it go for, say . . . thirty G.C.s?"

The mahm sniffed, then pulled in her eyestalks.

Tagg turned to the niblet. "Sorry, son. But you know what? Those gobbos over there wanted it." He nodded at a nest of nasty-faced Boyrs who were bashing their noggins with bungo fruits. "I'm sure they'll share the khokolatt. Of course, they might make you beg . . ."

"Mahm!" the niblet squealed.

The mahm's eyestalks wilted. "Oh, all right." She tapped her code into Tagg's account reader.

The niblet drifted away, his finagles clutching the game. "What a wonderful world."

Yes, it is, Tagg thought. Thirty G.C.s for a game that cost him only two, sold to him by a Xtran girl who had ballooned like a supernova after playing the game every day for a moon cycle. Her parents would have paid Tagg to take the game away, but heck, he was a fair trader. Fair but no one's sucker.

Thank the stars that they were filled with suckers, always looking to empty their pockets. And what was wrong with that? *Let the buyer take care*—that was Tagg's motto.

It was the buyer's job to care, not Tagg Orion's.

"Youch!" A bolt of pain shot through Tagg's eardrum.

"You should be ashamed of yourself!" Squeeto Burroe shrieked. "That stupid game will make that niblet sick!"

18

"So what? By the time he's puking up his precious snickerbootles, we'll be halfway across the galaxy."

"Promises, promises," Squeeto said with a huff.

Tagg had thought it would be easy credits, transporting the next-to-nothing Squeeto to Leo Minor. That was a big mistake, assuming a Burroe would be no trouble and all profit.

"Make yourself at home," Tagg had said. He had never dreamed that Squeeto would take up residence on his head! Squeeto was smaller than a speck but he had a mouth bigger than a pulsar. Always sticking his puny nose into Tagg's business.

"What's that smell?" Squeeto asked. "Did you have puffbeans for lunch again?"

"Me? What about your big mouth? You're probably sniffing your own blowback!"

The stink wafted through the marketplace, a thick odor of anger-sweat and hero-swagger. A Spyder extended his scent ports from his navel. The Aquarian mahm tipped her head back and spun her stalks. Even the Boyrs stopped their rowdiness and wrinkled their trunks.

"Blast!" Tagg grabbed his credit counter and started running.

"What! What's wrong?" Squeeto asked.

"Don't you know Dinn Tauro when you smell him?" Tagg hustled for the Launch Shelf. He left some great merchandise behind, but he didn't have time to cry over lost boola boops. Not when a smoke-sweating, rock-chewing lunatic was on his tail.

The Tauro was on the far side of the market, his paws wrapped around the three throats of a Vegan jeweler. Dinn Tauro looked like a mild-mannered LibraRian with his big eyes and floppy ears. But under that quacker-fuzz hair there were muscles of steel, the heart of a serpent, and the temper of a tornado.

"Tagg Orion! You pus-loving, snot-eating son of a Loapher!" Dinn bellowed.

"Great to see you again, Dinn. Sorry I can't stay and chat. Have a nice day!" Tagg ducked under a display of tentacle bracelets. The Launch Shelf was just a few rows away now, gleaming with ships of every size and shape.

Dinn Tauro's vessel was there, still glistening from its trip through the Inter-Dimensional Wheel. Shaped like a plain brown keg, *The Eliminator* looked like a harmless kegger. But Tagg knew better. Dinn Tauro had conquered fifty planetary systems in that ugly hulk of a ship. And he hadn't done it with his sweet smile.

Alongside Dinn's blaster were the usual local flitters— tiny vessels for planet hopping. Then, like a shining jewel, there was the *Bargain Hunter*. Crystal green and sleek, Tagg's ship was almost within linking distance.

"Hurry up!" Squeeto squeaked.

Tagg grabbed the remote from his pocket and pressed his code. Nothing. He wasn't close enough yet to link out of the here-and-now.

"Tagg Orion, you swine-smelling, sewer-sniffing fungus! Stop!"

Phomp! Hot air coursed through the market. A warning ripple—the laser blast would follow in seconds.

Tagg jammed the remote over and over as he ran, praying to be within range of the link-transfer field.

Rip! A white light swallowed Tagg and Squeeto and—

—they tumbled into cool. It was perfect nothing and perfect peace, if you were willing to give up your dreams and float forever—

—they emerged inside the *Bargain Hunter.*

"Go go go!" Squeeto yelled.

Tagg hit the launch button. Within microfolds, measured by realities rather than time, the *Bargain Hunter* was swept onto the Inter-Dimensional Wheel, sailing into the wonder and mystery that were the stars.

3

Sean had blown the whole day. Exploring the Arts. Persuading his parents to send him to the museum school. Capturing *Olivia Rising*.

He struggled until his brain was about to burst, but he could come up with only one option: Give up. Sean would grow up to be such a productive citizen that no one would even notice that his soul had starved to death.

Was there an Option Two? What would Franklin Zarkoff say? Frank had been neighbor, mentor, friend—and glassblower extraordinaire. Sure, Frank drove a junk of a car and he didn't always have a working phone or cable TV. But Frank had two furnaces, a garage full of tools, and vision beyond imagining.

No one limited Franklin Zarkoff's options.

Option Two: Don't give up! If Ms. Flack wouldn't allow him to be a glassblower and his parents wouldn't send him to the museum school, Sean would find his own way.

All he needed was good glass and good fire. The Dumpster at Crane's Neck Beach overflowed with bottles and jars. Made of soda lime, supermarket glass wasn't exactly *good* glass but it sure as heck was the cheapest kind of glass. Cheap? Heck, it was free if you didn't mind digging through mounds of trash to get to it.

Once Sean got glass, he would find good fire. Then he would astound the art world with his amazing technique and incredible vision. His parents would have to respect him when he became a famous artist. Maybe Olivia would even forgive him for laughing her off the beach.

But first he had to hold his nose, swallow his pride, and climb into the garbage.

An hour later, Sean crawled out of the Dumpster. His trash bag was filled with beer, wine, and soda bottles, and pickle and salsa jars. Now that he had a full supply of scrap glass, he needed to figure out where he would get fire. It wasn't like he could blow glass over a candle. A glassblower's furnace is as hot as the surface of the Sun.

Maybe he could use one of his father's blowtorches. Sean could work after school every day, before his parents got home. They'd think he'd given up the whole glass-blowing thing. When Monadnock Museum School begged him to go there, they would come around.

"That's the only place for a kid as gifted as our boy," his mother would say.

"Most artists starve," his father would add. "But our son is going to be the exception because he is so exceptional."

Sean leaned into the breeze, letting it sweep away the stink of garbage. The waves licked the sand with a steady whisper. Maybe he would make a wave—melt some green glass, blow an oval, then shape it with a crest. He could bubble it with tiny specks of gold, like stars swimming in the mighty ocean.

Stars Rising, Sean would call it. He would never sell it; he would give it to Olivia. Maybe she would give him a second chance.

Dark clouds rose from the east, blanketing out the stars on the horizon. The wind picked up. Cold rushed over Sean. He shivered, suddenly feeling very small.

What was he thinking? Great art wasn't going to come from trash and a blowtorch! Maybe his father was right. Maybe artists do starve. Maybe that's why Sean felt so empty now.

He collapsed onto the beach, too tired and too cold to move. It was easier just to sit here, watching the sand disappear under the water and the sky disappear under the clouds.

His hand brushed against something in the sand. Glass

shards—it looked like the lens from the eyepiece of Olivia's telescope. She must have broken it when she jammed her telescope into the case, trying to get away from him.

You screwed up again, Sean thought.

He trickled sand through his fingers. Sand was silica —the tiniest of glass creations, but mighty enough to hold back the oceans. Little specks that added up to something great.

Sean was a little speck, but he added up to nothing. Even the stars were little specks, disappearing under those heavy clouds. A chill worked through his bones, settling into his chest like a block of ice. The spark in his heart was going out and he couldn't do a stupid thing about it.

Then, in a blinding flash—the sky caught fire.

The *Bargain Hunter* swung like a yo-yo, bouncing Tagg and his cargo from one side of his ship to the other. Squeeto scurried across Tagg's face, digging in his toes with each lurch. "What's happening to us?" the Burroe cried.

"That idiot Dinn Tauro shot us off the Inter-Dimensional Wheel," Tagg said. "We've crashed on some nowhere planet." The ship flip-flopped again, and Tagg's stomach tumbled with it. There was a reason he had taken to the stars instead of sailing on the vast waters of his own planet. Seasickness.

"You promised to get me to Leo Minor!" Squeeto said.

"I'm sorry."

"You're apologizing? I thought Tagg Orion never apologized."

"So what? You want me to say I'm sorry for being sorry?" Tagg said.

"No, it's just that—I suppose we can be grateful that at least we're alive. Where are we?"

"Who knows? The *Bargain Hunter* isn't suited for falling through an atmosphere! The entry fused our sensors and melted our exit ports," Tagg said.

The computer spewed bad news so fast Tagg could barely process it. Every outside sensor—temperature, pressure, air, ability to sustain life—was reported as non-functional.

"What do we do now?" Squeeto yowled.

"I don't know!" Tagg said. He had never bargained for this—being held a prisoner in his own ship, which in turn was held prisoner by a violent and unknown ocean.

A brilliant flash tore through the clouds. Then, as quickly as they had come, the flames were swallowed by the ocean. The only light came from the crescent moon, floating on the waves.

Lights out, Sean thought. He tossed the bag of bottles back into the Dumpster, then took a last look at the water.

There it was again, a glint of light, rising on the crest of the wave, then disappearing in the trough. Wasn't that backward? The moon should be visible when the water flattened, then be blotted out when the waves rose higher on the horizon.

Something must be in the water.

Sean ran back to the shoreline. The shining object was about ten feet off the sand. The tide was moving out. The current would carry anything caught in it far out to sea.

Why should he care? It was probably just another piece of trash. A dented can catching light from the parking lot. Maybe a little kid's glow stick left over from Halloween. He should just go home.

Instead, he kicked off his sneakers and ran into the ocean.

The bottle felt alive in Sean Winger's hands.

Even though it had come out of the icy ocean, it was warm. About fifteen inches long, the bottle had an oval base, a rounded body, and a thick neck. The surface was ornate, textured with flowing lines and raised ridges.

Sean expected to find the bottle sealed with wax or a

cork, with a note inside—that whole message-in-a-bottle thing. But the end was fused shut, as if the artist wouldn't let his masterpiece be used for something as common as wine or perfume.

Finder's keepers—this amazing bottle now belonged to him.

When Sean walked into the kitchen twenty minutes later, he found his father washing dishes. Geoff Winger sniffed, then backed away. "What's that stench?"

"Just some leftover eau de gym. I didn't get a chance to take a shower at school. I'll grab one now." Sean was halfway down the hall when his father called him back.

"About this school business," his father said. "I know you're really into your hobby, but I only want what's best for you. We're trying to keep you focused."

"Focused on what you want, Dad. Not what I want."

"And what is it you want?" his father asked.

"You know what I want! I want to be a glassblower as great as Frank."

"I know how much you liked Franklin Zarkoff," his father said.

Liked? Sean had worshipped the old man. Frank's back had been bent from a lifetime at the furnace. But he saw something no one else could—and he knew it was good. He was only sixty-four when cancer swallowed him up.

Sean's chest ached when he thought about how much life could stink.

"Mr. Zarkoff was a talented man," his father continued. "But he struggled all his life to make ends meet. You need to know—"

"I know it all already," Sean snapped. "You've drilled it into me."

Glassblowing is no way to make a living. You can't live on dreams. Franklin Zarkoff is filling your head with nonsense. We want better for you. We want you to be safe.

"Because we know what's best for you," his father said.

"What's best for me right now is a shower," Sean said. He went into the bathroom and slammed the door.

By the time Sean had cleaned up and changed into sweats, his parents had already gone to bed. They truly believed the early bird got the worm. *Why settle for worms when you can have the stars?* Sean wondered.

He sneaked out to the garage. Before setting up the acetylene torch, he made sure his safety mask was snug and his insulated gloves and apron were secure. When the gas was flowing smoothly, he clicked the striker to spark a flame. The flame flared red, then blue.

The glass was the green of the ocean on a hot summer afternoon—the green you see when you open your eyes underwater and look up at the sun. *Maybe I shouldn't melt it*, Sean thought. *Maybe it would be wrong to destroy such incredible art.*

But how much had the original artist cared, to toss his bottle into the ocean? Sean had to believe he could make something even more incredible.

He put the bottle to the flame.

4

Squeeto nipped Tagg's eyelid. *"Wake up!"*

"Youch!" Tagg jerked upright and hit his head on the control panel. "Now what?"

"Look!" The ship's wall glowed red. "We're burning up! How is this happening? I thought we were in an ocean," Squeeto said.

"It might be an ocean of hot lava. Boiling oil. With the sensors fused, who knows?"

"We have to call for help!"

"We can't! Our communication ports are melted shut!" Tagg snapped.

"Then scream!" Squeeto yelled. "Bang! Make noise! Maybe whatever is burning us will hear us and stop."

Tagg dragged himself up from the floor and into his cargo bays. "Somewhere, I have . . . ah, here's the little clobber." Tagg upended a box of lawn bowlers. He aimed them all at the outside wall, set the spitter to HI, and pressed ON.

Bam! Bam! The bowlers blasted the wall. But the hot

31

spot continued to grow.

Tagg climbed another cargo shelf. "Where are they? I know I've got— Yes!" He yanked out a box of goober-bangs. He flung them, one at a time, against the outside wall. *Clunk! Clunk! Clunk!* The goobers would bang away for hours.

But the hot spot still spread. Tagg pounded the hull with his fists. "Help! There's intelligent life in here! Get us out!"

"Intelligent?" Squeeto echoed. "If you had a brain in your head, we wouldn't be in this mess."

Tagg pounded harder. "If you don't like it, leave."

"Help!" Squeeto bellowed into Tagg's middle ear.

Tagg was tempted to take his fist to his own head, just to shut the Burroe up. But while he had junk to sell and worlds to see, he was going to do whatever it took to get out of this mess. So he pounded and screamed—all the time watching the hot spot swallow his ship.

The bottle glowed orange, then red. This was the most awesome part—the moment when the glass started to flow, the moment when anything was a possibility.

Crack! No! It couldn't be. Sean backed the bottle out of the flame. He must have just imagined—

Crack! Crack! Crack! The sound every glassblower fears—

Sean soaked an old *Financial Times* with water and threw it over the bottle. The paper steamed, then smoldered. He waited the longest five minutes of his life before he unwrapped the newspaper. The bottle was still in one piece. And it was still *cracking*.

Sean fingered the glass. Each turn, curve, and texture felt so alive that he almost forgot he was looking for a flaw. He touched and rubbed and—

Bang!

"What's happening?" Squeeto yelled. Tagg jammed his remote but he was too late. Something was pulling them from outside, and there was nothing he could do except—

—*Tagg and Squeeto tumbled into cool. It wasn't air; it wasn't space. It wasn't anything, though it felt free and fine, the perfect nowhere that led to everywhere—*

—tumble onto a stone floor. *What a primitive hovel,* Tagg thought as he got up. Wood, concrete, and shingles were obsolete in the Amalgamation. So where had they fallen?

And who was this, this red-cheeked humanoid that howled at him? Slowly, the universal language chip in his brain made the strange squeals comprehensible. The humanoid was a *boy,* according to the chip's interpretation.

"Hi, there!" Tagg said.

"Um . . . hi, there," the boy answered. His eyes were as blue as Frikoo's moon. His hair was a rare shade of muddy brown. The boy's curls would fetch a nice price on Clostridia. Those egg noggins were always looking for bizarre head coverings.

Tagg was surprised to count five fingers on each of the boy's hands. Even though Tagg himself had five, most humanoids had at least six. But it wasn't the boy's hands that were important. It was what was *in* the boy's hands that startled Tagg.

Tagg's ship—the *Bargain Hunter*.

Sean Winger's heart pounded hard enough to break his ribs. Where had this guy come from? He was dressed like a pirate with a loose shirt, snug pants, and high boots. With his long blond hair and grass-green eyes, he looked like a movie star.

But even movie stars just don't appear out of nowhere. What were all those old tales and legends? When you rub a bottle, you get— "A genie!" Sean gasped.

"A genie? No, I'm an Ori—!" The genie grabbed his ear as if his eardrum had just exploded. He rubbed the side of his face, looking distracted, almost as if he were listening to his own thoughts.

When he finally smiled, it was as if the Sun had come

out. "Guilty as charged. I'm a genie."

"Holy Toledo!" Sean yelped. "Do you have a name?"

"Tagg Orion. You?"

"Sean Winger." Sean stuck out his hand to shake.

"Hey!" the genie shouted. "Two hands!"

"Huh?"

"Hold my sh—that thing with two hands! If you break it, you'll kill me."

"Sorry," Sean said. "I didn't know."

"There's a lot you don't know."

"True," Sean said. "But I do know this: because I freed you from your bottle, you have to give me whatever I ask."

Tagg Orion held up his hand. "Slow it down there, partner. You only get a few wishes. Don't blow the batch on snickerbootles and lollibams."

"Huh? What are snicker-whoosies and whatsie-bams?"

"Call it genie candy," the genie said. "You don't want to blow your few wishes on candy. Or maybe you do?"

"It depends. How few is few?"

Tagg tapped the side of his head as if shaking loose an answer. "Three wishes are traditional. Take some time, think them out. Wishing can be tricking."

"I don't need time!" Sean said. "I know exactly what I want." Good fire and good glass. Fame, fortune, and contentment would come when he mastered his art.

But the genie could be right. Maybe he should think

35

this through. What if he asked for a hot fire and the genie made his house burn down? If he asked for a fully equipped glassblowing studio in his backyard, his parents would refuse to let him use it.

Sean was just too tired to think straight. "Okay, Tagg," he said. "I do need some time. So let's sleep on it. Assuming genies do sleep."

Tagg Orion grinned. "You bet, Sean Winger. Now, if you don't mind, I'll hop back in the . . . bottle. After we both have a good night's rest, we'll discuss your wishes. But there's one more thing."

"What's that?"

"I need you to promise me that you will not show the bottle to anyone. And you'll hide it in a safe place."

"Why? Are you in trouble?" Sean asked. How many times had he been warned about strangers? And what was stranger than some guy popping out of a bottle?

"Me? Of course not! But I am in demand. Who wouldn't want three wishes?"

"A good point. Okay," Sean said.

"You have to swear on all things sacred," Tagg said. "I need to know I can trust you, or the wishes won't work."

"Okay, already." Sean tucked the bottle under his left arm, then raised his right hand. "I swear on Franklin Zarkoff's good name that I will keep your bottle safe."

"It's a deal!" Tagg Orion grabbed what looked like a

television remote that hung around his neck. "Sweet dreams, Sean Winger." With a twiddle of his fingers and a *whoosh*, he was gone.

Sean couldn't wait to get to sleep. He had big dreams to dream.

Come morning, he would tell the genie Tagg Orion exactly how to make those dreams come true.

5

Tagg Orion's feet felt like mashed bungos. He had been walking for three hours and hadn't found one open marketplace. The stores were locked but their windows teased midnight shoppers with well-lit displays. "You can look but you can't buy," they seemed to say.

"Look at these primitive clothes," Tagg said. "I haven't seen buttons since that estate sale on Granada."

"The footwear is secured with strings and buckles," Squeeto added. "Like objects of torture."

"Do you . . . um . . . I mean, your size and all . . ." Tagg stuttered. "Do you wear clothes?"

"You just said clothes were primitive."

"But what—" Tagg shut up. There were some things it was better not to know.

The next store's window was crammed with balls and sticks—universal toys except on underwater planets. Another store featured books and magazines. Tagg's two hearts hammered with excitement. Jeebers on a hundred planets would pay big credits for these antiquities!

A cold wind blew, making strange bumps on Tagg's arms. He shivered, a sensation the language chip called *goose bumps*. Climate control was obviously nonexistent here.

"What do you need to fix the ship?" Squeeto asked.

"This and that," Tagg said. Though Sean Winger had opened the ship from the outside, they still had problems. The *Bargain Hunter's* I-D launch circuitry was burned out, and Tagg didn't have a clue how to fix it.

"We might as well go back to the boy's home," Squeeto said. "These stores won't be open until daylight."

"When the Winger kid will be expecting me to deliver on his three wishes," Tagg said. "You realize the mess you've gotten us in?"

"Me? You're the one masquerading as a genie."

"Yeah, well, you're the one who fed me the information. Besides, it was the Winger boy's idea. And it's an easier explanation than the truth."

"Ah yes, the truth," Squeeto said. "Something to which you have a distinct aversion."

"I have an aversion to pain and suffering! Do you know what they do to extraterrestrials on this planet?"

"Enlighten me," Squeeto said.

"Sometimes they blow you up with atomics," Tagg said.

"No!" Squeeto gasped.

"If they capture you alive, they take you to this place in their desert where they stuff you with tubes, then cut you open! It's called Area 51."

"But the boy seemed so amicable," Squeeto said.

"Yeah. He had some nice junk in his room, didn't he?" Tagg said.

"You can't judge a person by his junk!" Squeeto snapped. "You never learn, do you, Tagg?"

"If you don't like it, why don't you go to Leo Minor?"

"Why don't you take me there? Like you promised? Like I paid for?"

"I don't know what's so good about Leo Minor anyway that you had to leave—" Where had he picked Squeeto up? He had been with him for so long, Tagg had forgotten.

A door opened in one of the buildings. Tagg watched as a man grabbed two barrels and pushed them to the street. Half asleep, the man stumbled back into the building without even noticing Tagg.

A lid slipped off one of the barrels with a clatter. Tagg stepped into the street to pick it up. As he replaced it, he glanced inside to see what the barrel contained.

Junk!

Tagg grinned. *One jeeber's junk is another jeeber's treasure,* he always said. This barrel was a dream come true.

Dinn Tauro dreamed the night away.

Mr. Goblie was uglier than any gutter rat, and a million times meaner. "Is your homework done, young sprout?"

"I left it in my locker," Dinn mumbled.

"This is your locker, young man." Mr. Goblie whacked the palm of his own hand with a ruler. "Where is your homework!"

"Um . . . the rat ate it?" Dinn stammered.

Whack! *Mr. Goblie's hand flew off and popped Dinn against the head. Mr. Goblie pointed his stump to a desk in the middle row. "Sit down!"*

Dinn scurried to sit. Mr. Goblie nodded to the front. "Now pay attention!"

A Gibber with three heads stood at the blackboard, spouting gibberish. Since the rat had chewed off Dinn's hand, he raised Mr. Goblie's hand instead. "Excuse me, but could you repeat that?"

The Gibber flung a notebook at Dinn. It bounced off his head and landed on his desk. "I am your FINAL EXAM!" the notebook proclaimed.

All gibberish! Dinn waved Mr. Goblie's hand, trying to get the Gibber's attention. But the Gibber had one head stuck in a book, another head stuck out the window, and the third head poked in a pencil sharpener, whittling his nose.

"You've got to listen to me!" Dinn cried. "I went to the wrong class all semester. I should have been coming here and learning how to ring dreams! Instead, I've been tagging

Orions off wheels! Please don't make me take this exam! I'm just not ready."

The Gibber turned all his heads toward Dinn. One head giggled. Within seconds, the other two heads joined the laughter. The Gibber laughed so hard and so long that he laughed his three fool heads off.

Olivia Ricci dreamed the night away.

A light split the sky like a flaming sword. Fire glowed on the ocean, sweeping up and down on the waves until it crashed ashore in a pinwheel of sparks.

A figure stepped out of the sea. With flowing blond hair and deep green eyes, he might be considered a handsome man. But Olivia knew two things: that handsome doesn't count for puffbeans and that the stranger was not a man. He was a visitor to Earth. And he had come just for her.

Olivia took his hand. She felt no fear, only a great anticipation of the adventure that lay beyond. As she stepped out of the Sun and into the Universe, she heard her mother calling for her.

"Olivia! I expect you home by eight thirty."

"I might be a little late," Olivia called back. "But only by a light-year or two."

Sean Winger dreamed the night away.

Sean's face ached from smiling. He had never realized that receiving universal acclaim and praise would be such hard work. "Thank you," he said to yet another critic who could find nothing to criticize and everything to praise about the Winger collection.

Olivia pushed through a knot of critics and fans. "Winger, you need your caviar!"

A waiter with blond hair and eyes the color of summer grass trailed behind her. "Master. You need to keep up your strength if you want to grow up to be famous," he said.

Sean eyed the black mass on the crisp bread. Was this the price of success? You had to eat roadkill? "Why did you bring me this?"

"That's what you wished for," the waiter said.

"But it stinks! Like something you scraped out of the trash," Sean protested.

"Garbage in, garbage out." The waiter touched his neck and disappeared.

Then everyone disappeared, leaving Sean alone with Olivia. Her midnight-blue dress sparkled with silver. Her hair gleamed like the Sun starting a new day. Her eyes were so dark they could see what never could be and what always was.

Sean Winger might be a world-famous artist, but he was a fool to think he could capture Olivia Ricci's fire.

"What fire?" Olivia whispered. "Don't you remember? You laughed my fire out. Like this." The stars in her dress winked out one by one. "Like me." She faded into a blue mist.

"Where are you going?" Sean cried.

"Where they believe in me," she said, disappearing in a spark.

Sean was alone. But not really alone. The gallery was filled with the work of his hands. Paperweights veiled with spun gold. Enameled vases the color of winter skies. Crystal horses. Flowing waterfalls. A rainbow of pitchers, plates, and ornaments. He closed his eyes and breathed in the smell of success.

The stench was suffocating!

Sean opened his eyes. The Winger collection had been drowned in a ton of garbage! "What the heck!" he yelled. "Who slimed my stuff?"

A rat scurried over mounds of diapers. Behind him, Sean heard a whoosh. More rats, bigger than the first, ate moldy pizza off his Grecian lace plates.

"What are you doing here?" he yelled.

"We caught the early worm!" The rats laughed, sounding like an army of weed whackers.

When they were finished gobbling, there was nothing left. No trash, no rats, no lifetime of great art.

Only the stifling stench of rotting garbage.

6

When Sean opened his eyes, he was surrounded by mounds of plastic bags and stacks of newspapers. Had he fallen asleep in the Dumpster?

He pried his eyes open all the way. It was his bedroom, filled with morning light and trash. Was last night just a dream—and this morning the nightmare?

"Whoops!" A voice, sounding like a mouse with a megaphone, shook him fully awake.

"Shut up, Squeeto," Tagg whispered.

The genie was climbing in through his bedroom window! The guy had a lounge chair on his back and one of Dorothy Winger's lawn trolls tucked under each arm.

"Who's Squeeto?" Sean said. "And what's all this trash doing in my room?"

"You should thank me," Tagg said. "I cleaned the streets of your town!"

"Are you nuts?" Sean yelped. Various items from the neighborhood littered his floor. Rick's skateboard. Nicole's softball bat. Mr. Todd's fertilizer spreader. The bird feeder from Mrs. Joslyn's garden. A bicycle pump. A plastic Santa Claus. A pooper-scooper.

"I try to do a good deed and I get insulted? I don't have to stay here and take this abuse." Tagg Orion wrapped his fingers around the remote that he had used to get into the bottle last night.

"Oh, no, you don't!" Sean leaped at the genie, grabbing his shirt and—

—*Sean tumbled into cool. It wasn't anyplace he had been before, but he thought it might be a nice place to stay, suspended forever in a haze of velvet and nothing*—

—and landed in a heap on a floor. A floor that glowed green. It was neither wood nor stone but hard just the same. Hard, and somehow alive.

Like glass is alive.

"The bottle." Sean gasped. "I'm inside the bottle." Sean yanked away from Tagg, then began to run, panic clawing in his belly.

The bottle might be only fifteen inches or so long on the outside, but the inside was bigger than a gymnasium. Rows of shelves crowded the center of the bottle, like a superstore. Every spare inch of space was crammed with junk.

Sean recognized toys, dishes, books, appliances. Some things were only vaguely familiar, like a chair that was wide enough for an elephant and a computer with an

46

octagonal screen. Other things were downright bizarre. A plastic tube twisted into multiple figure eights. A wooden block covered with what looked like fuzzy mushrooms. Jeweled rings, big enough to fit a moose, hung off loops.

What was Tagg Orion doing with all this junk? *This must be how he makes wishes come true,* Sean realized. It wasn't magic. It was inventory!

Sean ran down a row crammed with magazines and books. He scrambled halfway up a shelf, then slid in as far back as he could. He needed to hide, to think this out. What would Tagg Orion do to him now that Sean had invaded his bottle? Sean didn't know beans about genies.

The magazines! Maybe they would give him a clue. Sean grabbed a few out of a nearby pile, then silently paged through them. The pages were filled with imps, ghouls, and monsters. These couldn't be genies! Some creatures had two heads, some had flaming skin, some had eyes covering every part of their bodies.

The flaming creatures lived in rocky caves with multiple chimneys. A sack of bug-eyed vomit lived in what seemed to be a running sewer. Tiny crabettes with four heads and razor claws lived in the fur of lumbering cows. But what kind of cows were these, with five legs, two tails, and their heads on sideways?

The artwork was incredibly precise, as if the images had been produced by a camera. But cameras record only reality. These pictures were too bizarre, too absurd to be real.

Sean heard footsteps. Seconds later, Tagg yanked him off the shelf. "Gotcha!"

Sean backpedaled, trying to get away. What if he had really ticked off the genie by invading his bottle? What if Tagg was going to turn him into something gross, like walking snot?

But then again, had he actually seen Tagg Orion do magic? If he could make things appear out of thin air, then what did he need all this junk for?

Sean jerked out of Tagg's grasp and backed against the wall.

"Hey, don't be afraid," Tagg said with that sunshine smile. "Genies don't bite."

"Who said you were a genie?" Sean said.

"Why, you did," Tagg said. "Don't you remember?"

Hairless and sneering, genies carried curved swords and wore funny shoes. With his long blond hair, buff shoulders, and pirate clothes, Tagg Orion looked like a hero. A regular old Hercules. Or a Sinbad. Or a Han Solo.

Han Solo who zipped around the galaxy in a space-ship.

Sean's knees went wobbly. What had Olivia said? *The possibilities are so endless that they become probable.*

Fire in the sky. A bottle in the water. Tagg Orion in

the bottle. "You're not a genie at all!" Sean gasped.

"Then what am I?" Tagg asked.

"You're an extraterrestrial from outer space," he said. "An alien in a bottle!"

"Bingo!" that loud voice shouted out of nowhere.

Tagg just yawned. "Well, Sean Winger. Looks like you can kiss those three wishes good-bye."

Sean's dreams crashed in on him like some sick, cosmic joke. When he needed the Universe to give him a break, it coughed up an alien instead.

Sean had seen all those movies. Most aliens, especially those who lie and steal, are up to no good. Today Tagg was after lawn trolls; tomorrow it could be military secrets or the Earth's whole ecosystem.

He had to tell someone! But first, he had to get out of this bottle or ship or whatever it was.

Sean grabbed the remote from around Tagg's neck.

"Hey, what do you think you're doing?" Tagg yelled.

"I'm going back to my planet! Then I'm going to turn you in to the authorities!"

"No!" Tagg gasped. "You don't want to do that!"

"Yes, I do!" Sean tried to sound brave, but his guts pushed through his tonsils.

"Don't you care what happens to me?" Tagg whined.

"Why should I? I don't even know you," Sean said.

"Tell him!" that invisible voice boomed.

A speck flashed across Tagg's nose, so tiny and quick that Sean thought he had imagined it. "What's that? A bug?" Sean asked.

"A Burroe." Tagg sighed. "Squeeto Burroe, to be exact."

"What's a Burroe?"

"A loudmouthed, opinionated freeloader," Tagg said.

"I'd rather be loud than slippery," the speck boomed. "I'd rather be opinionated than butt-kissing. I'd rather be a freeloader than a conniving, scheming shuckster."

"See what I have to endure?" Tagg looked at Sean like he expected sympathy.

The speck settled on Tagg's nose. Sean leaned closer, trying to see the Burroe.

Tagg ripped the remote out of his hand. "Gotcha again!"

"Yeah, you got me. So, what are you going to do with me?" Sean forced a laugh, but he was so scared now he could sneeze his guts out of his sinuses. "Cut me into pieces? Cook me for supper? Or maybe you'll just put me in a zoo for all your bug-eyed buddies to throw peanuts at."

"We wouldn't do that. The Amalgamated Planets are civilized," Squeeto said. "But here on Earth, your authorities kidnap courteous visitors and ship them to this scumhole called Area 54—"

"That's Area 51," Tagg said.

"Area 51 doesn't exist," Sean said.

"Bingo!" Squeeto Burroe yelped. "Neither do aliens. But here we are."

"What the heck are you doing here?" Sean asked. Were Tagg Orion and his big-mouthed flea scouting for an alien invasion?

"A stray power blast damaged my ship and dropped us on your planet," Tagg said.

"So why don't you just ask for help?" Sean asked. "NASA? The FBI?"

"Your planet isn't part of the Amalgamation," Squeeto explained. "If we made ourselves public, even if your people didn't ship us off to Area 51, there would be severe consequences."

"From the FBI?" Sean asked.

"From the Amalgamation," Tagg said.

"You said your Amalgamation was civilized!"

"And intent on staying that way. Even if it means a" — Squeeto paused— "a cleanup operation."

Every pulp scifi movie Sean had ever seen reran in his head. All the endings were the same—bad news for somebody, be they pasty-faced Earthlings or lizard-headed aliens. "So what do you want from me?" he asked.

"You promised you'd hide my ship," Tagg said.

"I promised I'd hide your bottle," Sean replied.

"Same thing," Tagg said. "You need to keep it safe while I fix it."

"Why should I?" Sean asked.

"Because I'll give you anything you want out of my cargo," Tagg said. "Anything!"

His parents had warned him a million times about strangers. Besides, junk offended Sean's artistic sensibility. "No offense," he said. "But I'm not interested."

"Why not? I have the best junk in the Universe," Tagg said. "Just tell me what you want."

"My three wishes would have been nice." Sean sighed.

"What would you have wished for?" Squeeto said.

"Good fire and good glass. That's all I need and that's all I want."

Tagg grinned. "Do I have a deal for you!"

Sean Winger looked into the face of the Sun. "Seriously? This is my Sun? The star that Earth orbits?"

Tagg had opened a door in his ship's control panel. Even though the door wasn't bigger than a foot square, the fierce light and powerful heat seemed to be endless. "Of course," Tagg said. "That's my current link to the Inter-Dimensional Wheel. At any point in time, we're linked to the closest star."

"But that's only inches away," Sean said. "The Sun is at least—" How many millions of miles? Olivia would know.

"Four thousand quadrants," Squeeto said. "In Earth terms, ninety-three million miles. But on the Inter-Dimensional Wheel, distance is irrelevant."

"What the heck is the Inter-Dimensional Wheel?"

"That's how we travel from one planetary system to another," Tagg said. "You didn't think we actually flew, did you?"

"How would I know?" Sean's head pounded. He didn't even know the capital of Bolivia. How could anyone expect him to know astrophysics?

"We don't travel through space," Squeeto said. "We move along Inter-Dimensional Spokes, linking through the dimensional folds in the center of each star—"

"Okay, whatever," Sean said. It was all awesome, but trying to unfold the Universe in his mind made him nauseous. He needed to get his bearings.

"What I really don't get is this," Sean said. "How can your ship be the size of a bottle on the outside and this big inside?"

Tagg scratched his head. "It just is."

"Don't think of this as a ship or any sort of moving vehicle," Squeeto said. "It's more like a containment vessel. It only has to be big enough to contain the link transfer."

"The link transfer? You mean the remote?" Sean asked.

"Bingo!" Squeeto said. "When you use it to transfer

from outside—in this case, your room—you fold into another dimension—in this case, the inside of Tagg's ship."

"So the inside is a thousand times bigger than the outside?"

"The outside is in normal space. But the inside of the bottle is not really inside. It's elsewhere, on a dimensional fold where space is irrelevant," Squeeto said.

"So my Sun is not really inside here but it's nearby, on a dimensional fold?"

"Clever boy!" Squeeto bellowed. "And we thought this planet was primitive."

"Speaking of your Sun—is that fire hot enough for you?" Tagg asked.

Franklin Zarkoff had said more than once that a glass-blower's furnace was as hot as the surface of the Sun. And here was the real thing, right within reach. "I suppose." Sean tried to keep his voice cool.

"Great!" Tagg beamed. "So we've got a deal."

"But I can't use it! Everyone knows you can't look directly into the Sun. I would burn my eyes out," Sean said.

"Primitive thinking," Tagg said, shaking his head. "The link is obviously shielded against radiation."

"It might be obvious to you, but it's not to me."

"Watch!" Tagg tapped a button on the control panel.

The ship was flooded with impossibly bright light for a split second, then returned to its normal hue. "That's the unshielded Sun. The shield protects us from all that. So—do we have a deal?"

"Not yet." This could be the biggest screwup of Sean's life, hiding an alien spaceship. Everything had to be perfect or he couldn't agree to do this.

"Okay, I've got the fire. But I need glass," Sean said. "Good glass—not soda lime stuff like I got out of the Dumpster."

"Dumpster?" Tagg looked like he had just won the lottery. "Is that what I think it is?"

This guy was worse than a trash-picking dog! "Forget that," Sean snapped. "What about my glass? I want something fine. High-purity soda lime. Or better yet, borosilicate."

"Get him some glass," Squeeto snapped.

Tagg ran into his storage rows and pulled down a carton. "All I have are these cheap mugs from Shoftus. Each time a Shoftissi filled her fuel tanks at a dispensing station, she got a free cup."

Gas station giveaways, Sean thought. The cheapest kind of trash. He looked in the carton, expecting nothing.

It was like gazing into a treasure chest! Glass of every color and texture glittered like jewels. "It's a deal!" he shouted.

It was an amazing end to what had turned out to be a perfect day.

Sean Winger finally had good fire and good glass. And he didn't have to go to Monadnock Museum School to get it.

7

Squannacook Middle School had never looked so good. The walls were still goat vomit brown and the windows grimy gray. But Sean looked long past this dump of a school and into his shining future.

Yesterday he had crawled into a Dumpster searching for good fire and good glass. Today he had it. All because of an alien in a bottle, right in his backpack.

"Hey, Winger." Luke Chang shoved four pieces of grape gum into Sean's hand. "I need you to work this for me, man."

"Now?"

"I got kids working gum all day." Luke sucked back a yellow dribble that reeked lemon. "I've got to get the *Notre Gum Cathedral* finished by next week."

"What's the rush?" Sean asked, popping in two pieces. Grape gum was disgusting, but it was his duty to support a fellow artist.

Luke fished a flyer out of his pocket and handed it to him. "You know Ms. Flack. Too busy making eyes at

Mr. Vincent to remember to give this to us until the last possible second."

HOLLIS ART FAIR—Saturday, March 24
Entries now being accepted for the
Youth Division (ages 12–16)
First prize: Full scholarship to
Monadnock Museum School

"I'm going to win," Luke said, grabbing the flyer back. He walked away, blowing a yellow bubble.

"No you're not," Sean said quietly. "I am."

Olivia dreaded science class that morning.

Perhaps for the first time in her life, Olivia didn't have the homework assignment complete. It was all Winger's fault. If he hadn't laughed at her last night, she wouldn't have left it at Crane's Neck. She knew he wouldn't have it—Sean Winger was too creative and abstract to do anything routine like organize and turn in homework.

What a fool she had been! Maybe it was a valuable lesson. If Olivia couldn't trust a dreamer like Sean Winger to understand her, she would never be able to trust anyone.

Except for people from the stars—if they would ever

come! This would be the ideal moment for them to appear, before Mr. Johnson asked for her homework. Or before Sean came in and started laughing again.

Olivia pulled her science book from her backpack. She would tell Mr. Johnson that a cold front backed in off the ocean and she'd need tonight to finish her sketch.

The class was filling with kids. The cool boys laughed and shoved each other. The cool girls smiled and giggled. The studious kids sat down and organized their classwork.

Sean wandered in. In his black T-shirt and jeans, he looked drab next to the cool kids. But his eyes were always so alive, as if they saw something no one else could. And now, it felt like he was looking right through her.

Olivia folded her arms and lay her head down on her desk.

"Olivia!" he whispered.

She didn't move.

"Olivia! You're not going to believe this!"

"Believe what? That you're a total jerk?" The back of her neck flushed as if she had a fever.

"Believe that the *probability* has become a reality," he whispered.

Olivia opened one eye. "What are you talking about?"

"That thing—" Sean looked around to make sure no one else was listening. "That thing you said you're waiting for . . ."

"The only thing I'm waiting for is for you to leave me alone," Olivia said. She straightened in her seat and opened her book.

"But we're not alone! I know, because I found one last night," Sean said.

"Found what?" Olivia asked.

"An alien! You know the Dumpster at Crane's Neck. I was in there when—"

"The Dumpster? Stupid me! All that time I've spent looking at the stars when I should have been digging in the trash."

"You've got to believe me," Sean said. "I know I laughed last night—"

"Was that you laughing?" Olivia said. "Excuse me, I thought it was a donkey! Braying like a fool." She shoved her book into her backpack and headed for the front of the room.

Sean followed her. "I'm sorry," he cried. "I was ignorant! I didn't know then what I know now."

Their science teacher had just come in. "Mr. Johnson, may I be excused?" Olivia asked.

"Is something wrong?" Mr. Johnson asked.

"I have a headache." Olivia gave Sean the dirtiest look she could, then turned back to her teacher. "And it's becoming a royal pain in my neck."

Sean Winger disappeared in the middle of language lab. No one saw him go. It was simply a matter of closing the door to the booth, sliding down in his chair, and pressing the remote—

—*flying through that nothing that was everything, that nowhere that was everywhere*—

From Squannacook Middle School, through the link transfer, and into the bottle.

Tagg and Squeeto had gone out window-shopping. Sean hoped Tagg Orion had listened to his lecture on shoplifting. He didn't think his father would appreciate having to bail an extraterrestrial out of jail. Meanwhile, he had forty minutes to set up his glassblowing studio before Ms. Gomez came looking for him.

When Franklin Zarkoff died, he left everything he owned to Sean. But after Sean's father paid off Frank's creditors, all that was left were his hand tools: his blow-pipes, tongs, paddles, tweezers, shears, bashers, eye protectors, gloves, apron. And the one thing that no one could take away or sell—four years of training at the furnace.

The night before, Sean had rescued an old convection oven from his attic to use for annealing—the slow cooling of heated glass. You can't just work gas at two thousand degrees Fahrenheit, then let it set at room temperature. The varying thickness of the glass cools at different rates, causing the glass to crack and maybe explode. You have to cool glass over hours or days in an annealing oven to be safe.

Sean scrounged a metal table from Tagg's shelves to use as a marver for shaping hot glass. He set up everything near the ship's control panel, then checked his watch.

Thirty minutes left. Not enough to create a master-piece, but enough time to experiment. Sean studied the broken lens from Olivia's telescope. He could make one, he knew he could. He knew he should—Olivia was furi-ous with him. He had to do something to make her talk to him again.

The crucible shimmered with melted glass. Tagg had given him a lava lamp—spitting real lava—to use as a burner. Sean preheated the end of his blowpipe, then dipped it at a shallow angle into what used to be a Shoftissi mug. The glass glistened and stretched like hot caramel. Sean rotated the pipe quickly and contin-uously to keep it on the end of the pipe.

Then he opened the door to the Sun.

8

That night, Sean knew where to find Olivia. The same waves lapped the sand and the same stars hung in the sky. But in the twenty-four hours since Sean had climbed out of the Dumpster, his whole world had changed.

She sat on her blanket, staring at the March sky from under her winter jacket and earmuffs. Her telescope stood on its tripod, its eyepiece duct taped with a piece of glass.

He held out the lens. "I made this for your telescope. I'm sorry the other one broke last night."

Olivia looked at the lens like it was a piece of moldy seaweed. "Optical lenses are ground, not blown," she said. "Oh, I forget—you're the kid who doodles through science. You're not likely to understand the physics of refracted light."

"I don't know physics but I do know glass," Sean said. "Please. Try it."

Olivia sighed. She took the lens and slid it into the eyepiece.

"See? It fits!" he said.

"So you know how to use a ruler. That doesn't mean it will work."

"Of course it will," Sean said. *Please,* he prayed.

Olivia put her eye to the lens. She fiddled with the focus, then suddenly pulled away as if she had been stung by a hornet.

"What?" Sean said. "What's wrong?"

"Winger, what did you do?"

"I didn't do anything."

"Yes, you did." She pushed him to the telescope. He squinted, then focused. The sky danced with color!

"Holy cannoli," Sean said. Through the telescope, the stars were laced together with strands of color, as if a cosmic spider had spun a web of rainbows across the sky. Every few seconds, one strand or another would flicker with a point of light.

Sean looked away from the eyepiece, taking in the sky with his naked eye. The stars winked on, small grains of gold in a darkening sky. The moon nipped out of the waves and would soon outshine everything.

His own eye, even with his great artistic vision, could only see the usual night sky. What was different about the new lens? It was made with glass from outer space. Heck, outer galaxies! Somehow it must be showing what humans had never seen, never even knew existed—the

Inter-Dimensional Wheel!

"Olivia, it's like I've been trying to tell you! The visitors from the stars—this proves they exist!"

Olivia whipped the lens at him. "I should be complimented that you went to all this trouble to make fun of me." She took the scope off the tripod and began packing up.

"Olivia, please don't go. Please don't—"

What was that, out of the corner of his eye? Light glinted on the bluff, the grassy acres of wildlife preserve at the opposite end of Crane's Neck. "Olivia, look!"

She squinted. "Some jerk with a match, that's all."

Sean grabbed the eyepiece out of her telescope case. "Give me that back," Olivia snapped.

He slid the lens back in and sighted across the water. His breath caught in his chest and he had trouble getting words out. "You have to see this. It's . . . unbelievable."

Olivia folded her arms and turned away from him.

"Please, Olivia. Please look."

Olivia took the eyepiece and focused. Sean knew the sight had become clear when he heard her gasp.

The bluff was alive with Ferris wheels and roller-coasters!

9

Dinn Tauro needed to sleep more than he needed to breathe. He slung his fuzzer over his shoulder, tucked his head-stone under his arm, and prepared to go outside to the alien sand.

"Stay in the ship!" he ordered his crew. If he was going to spawn dreams that would consume his here-and-now, the least he could do was not endanger his ship and crew.

"But Your Loftiness," the Physician protested. "You'll be out there all alone, without us to protect you. What if you spawn something from your dreams that consumes you?"

Then I will finally be happy, Dinn Tauro thought.

That lie-spewing, trash-peddling Tagg Orion had promised that the Dream Ring would channel all Dinn's nightmares into the darkest dimension. Instead, the Dream Ring spun all of Dinn's deepest heartaches into this here-and-now, and gave them light-sucking, joy-ripping life.

Minutes later, surrounded by sand and sky, Dinn

settled his shaggy head down on the ground. The wind howled but Dinn Tauro felt no cold under his fuzzer. Hadn't he endured the lower poles of Egloo? That frost-burning, toe-chewing remnant of a red star had frozen the spit in their mouths. Dinn and his crew had prevailed by bellowing sprout rhymes until they thawed enough to hike to safety.

Sprout rhymes. Dinn hadn't thought of his sprout-hood in eons. Those were the days, when the wildest adventures were found in Scream Parks, riding on cardiac coasters—

—screaming his fool head off! When Dinn was beyond dizzy, he'd let go of the safety bar and fly without fear and without wings. A pink wall rose before him. Dinn stretched out his arms and prepared to meet his fate—

—then breathed in delight as his fate swallowed him! Cloud candy, spun from sweet blossoms and bird song, wrapped him in a fuzzy embrace. He ate and ate until every pore in his body burst with nectar.

And burst he did, into a firewheel of Dinns so he was all places at once. He rode the cardiac coaster, flew the pirouette, yo-yo-ed on the roundhouse, splashed through the waterspill. Dinn swirled in a cyclone of light, spinning off glee like sparks. Can this finally be happiness? *he wondered.*

If it is, I never want to wake up.

A carnival had sprung up on Crane's Neck Bluff. Lights flashed, rides whirled, and—

—someone screamed! That was a child howling across the water, a little boy! Olivia started running. Sean followed but the going was slow. The beach was a half mile long; the sand was heavy under their feet.

As they drew closer, the carnival took bizarre shape.

What had looked like a Ferris wheel from the far side of the neck was more of a giant pinwheel. The huge sphere, taller than a church spire, spun too fast to be fun or even safe. Instead of gentle bench seats, the rider would have to strap to one of the wheels that lined the outside of the globe. The wheels were lit like Christmas trees and spinning like tops.

"That's insane." Olivia panted. "A human body couldn't stand those g forces."

Another ride was a massive pendulum that swung in longer arcs until it made a complete circle. Then the pendulum opened its arms and flung its cars into the darkness.

The roller-coaster they had seen from a half mile down the beach now looked more like a gargantuan snake. The cars didn't just roll on the rails—the snake rail bed itself moved, writhing in vicious circles and loops.

As they got closer, the screaming grew louder. "The kid doesn't sound scared," Sean said. "I think he's having fun."

"He's supposed to be," Olivia said. "It's a carnival, isn't it?"

"Who knows?" he said. If a bottle could be a spaceship, then a carnival could be anything. Including a trap.

Dinn Tauro's fathers told tales of adventures beyond the stars. His mothers boasted of conquests beyond imagining. "The Universe awaits you, Little Loftiness," they promised.

Dinn twirled so fast he could see the years go by. His travels piled on him like colorless rocks, weighing him deeper into the Tauro unhappiness that sucked in laughter and spit out heroes.

What good is being a hero when you're so life-sapping, heart-breaking unhappy?

"No!" he protested. "I won't grow up! And you can't make me!" The mighty Dinn Tauro was a conqueror and he was a king. Surely he could turn back the hands of time. He yanked with all his might. The dark began to scatter and the light to shine.

Then he felt a gnawing.

Gutter rats, now shrunk to the size of mosquitoes, chewed at his fingers. Dinn wanted to shoo them away, but if he let go the hands of time, he knew he would cartwheel into a bottomless future. He hung on for dear life and dear happiness. He ignored the prickling in his fingers as a thousand tiny rats chewed away his chance at happiness.

His will endured but his fingers did not. They fell away, one by one, ground into the hands of time until Dinn hung on only by his nipper finger. The gutter rats chewed as one, a grating sound that signaled his last chance.

Last chance to be happy.

Sean and Olivia found the little boy clinging to the bottom of the snake coaster. More teddy bear than kid, he had huge brown eyes and fluffy black hair. He looked barely old enough to walk.

The ride was bucking and twisting, the cars whirling so fast that they could barely see them. The boy was only a couple of feet off the ground. If he let go, he would safely drop onto the sand.

"Why doesn't he let go?" Olivia said. The snake rail arched and suddenly the boy was airborne, a hundred feet over their head.

The cars rushed over the boy's hands. Sean's stomach lurched—was that a finger he saw flying off? The arching snake rail slowly relaxed and the boy lowered with it to the ground. His hands were bloody stumps. He hung on to the rails with his pinky finger.

"Let go!" Olivia yelled.

The boy howled loudly. What madness was this? He

had lost most of his fingers but still seemed to be having fun. The cars thundered at the far side of the snake rails. In a heartbeat, the snake rail would arch again.

"Let go!" Olivia screamed again.

"No!" the boy howled, this time in clear English. "No! No! No! You can't make me."

The snake rails began to rise. "Let go!" Sean hollered. He wrapped his arms around the boy.

"No!" he yelled. Even though he held on by one pinky, the boy carried Sean with him as his feet left the ground.

Olivia wrapped her arms around Sean's legs. "Winger! Make him let go!"

"He won't!"

They rose with the boy and the snake rail.

Suddenly, the boy's last little finger popped off. It was disgusting and tragic but a huge relief as they all tumbled onto the sand.

Olivia helped the boy up. "He's so light," she said. "He doesn't weigh anything."

He was so light that he was dissolving in a vapor of eyes and fuzz. "Why did you make me stop?" the boy whispered.

His last words lingered long after they couldn't see him anymore. "I was so happy."

Olivia peered under a merry-go-round that spun two-headed dragons and winged elephants. Minutes earlier, it had twirled a hundred feet in the air, the dragons belching smoke and the elephants flapping wings. "Where did that boy go? And where did this all come from?"

"I'm not sure. But I think Tagg might know," Sean said.

"Tagg who?" Olivia asked.

Sean was so nervous that he lapsed into speed-speak. "A little green man who's not little or green, except his eyes. He looks normal, but the guy who travels with him, this Squeeto Burroe, well, he's so small he's almost invisible. But what a mouth, he's always complaining. I pulled them out of the ocean last night. Well, not him but his ship. Which isn't really a ship, it's a bottle. Well, not exactly a bottle, it's a containment vessel. Anyway, this guy Tagg, the one with the green eyes, well, he's somewhat of a bragger and I guess even a bit of a liar. Kind of like a used car salesman, I'm thinking. He's—"

"Used car salesman?" Olivia laughed. "Is that the best you can do, Winger?"

"You think I'm lying?" His voice cracked from frustration.

"Not exactly lying. But you're an artist, right? So I think you invented this Tagg character to show me you can get into this whole outer space thing."

"I *am* into this whole outer space thing!" Sean shouted. "And I can prove it!"

"Forget it," Olivia said. "I never should have trusted you."

Sean watched as she walked away into the darkness.

Dinn Tauro raged at his crew. "The only good thing ever to come out of my dreams, and you had to laser it?"

The Physician spoke with measured tones. "Your Loftiness, we couldn't leave it for the natives to find. And it was too big to disassemble and bring into the ship."

Dinn drew his head-whacker. The Physician stood tall, prepared to sacrifice herself for her commander's displeasure. But Dinn simply howled, then jammed his whacker into the nearest bungo fruit.

"What can we do, Loftiness?" the Navigator asked.

"Are you certain that there is no way to remove this Dream Ring?" Dinn asked.

"No way," the Physician said. "At least, not without cutting off your head."

"I may be ready for that," Dinn said, leaning the head in question against the wall.

"We are not ready for that," the Sergeant-at-Arms said. She exchanged a worried glance with the Navigator. They had, of course, discussed that very solution.

"What is left for me, then? Except nightmares that stalk my sleep, then consume my waking world?" Dinn whispered.

"Revenge," the Sergeant-at-Arms said.

"Revenge," the Physician agreed. She knew that revenge was often more soul-soothing than glee.

"Revenge," the Waste Office chortled. That giant gutter rat in the trash hold was looking for a hardy meal, and Tagg Orion was the jeeber for the job.

"Revenge," the Physician chorused. "If you cannot rest, then we shall not rest until we find Tagg Orion."

His crew bobbed their heads vigorously. They did not know happiness but they knew determination and purpose—and this was such a moment.

Revenge would be sweet. Revenge would be certain. And Dinn Tauro vowed that revenge would be universal.

10

T he next morning, Tagg disavowed all knowledge of the carnival. "Not me," he said. "I had considered going into amusement work but there's too much overhead, not enough variety. Besides, I like to travel light."

Squeeto snorted like a broken muffler. "You call this light? The only reason this ship isn't stocked from top to bottom is because you don't have any Earth credits."

"And isn't that a shame?" Tagg sighed.

"Don't look at me," Sean said.

Tagg looked at him anyway. "Are you absolutely, positively sure you can't lend me any of your currency?"

"If I had any money, I wouldn't be digging in Dumpsters for glass. You want money, get a job."

Squeeto laughed, making a noise like a sputtering chipmunk.

"Real funny," Tagg said. "It's not like you work for a living, Squeeto."

"My needs are simple," Squeeto said. "Whereas you,

Tagg Orion, are quite the luxury item. Can you help get him a job, Sean Winger?"

Sean groaned, trying to imagine Tagg pumping gas or pushing papers. Who would hire a long-haired, slick-smiling huckster with no references and no résumé?

"I've got it!" Sean said. "My school cafeteria needs someone to work the line."

"What does that mean?" Tagg asked.

"Serve food to kids," Sean said.

"No way," Tagg said.

"He'll take it!" Squeeto yelled.

While Tagg sputtered, Squeeto and Sean made arrangements to sneak Tagg out of the bottle during gym class.

Then Sean hustled to get ready for school. He and Olivia had a lot to talk about—assuming she would consent to speak to him.

It was only when Sean was halfway to school that he realized he had forgotten to ask Tagg if there could be other aliens here on Earth.

Aliens who loved roller-coasters.

The head lunch lady, Mrs. Confrancisco, didn't even ask for a résumé. Tagg's bright smile and slick charm provided all the reference he needed. At noontime, Sean saw Tagg working hard—trading extra desserts for gel pens, breath mints, and rope bracelets.

"What are you doing?" Sean whispered.

"You know what they say," Tagg said. "One clobbo's pocket lint is another clobbo's treasure." Sean grabbed his tray and hustled out to the lunchroom. He had agreed to hide the bottle; no way was he going to baby-sit Tagg Orion, too.

Sean usually ate lunch with Luke, Susan, and the other EAP kids. The "artiste association," they called themselves. "Freaks," most everyone else called them. They wore either title with as much pride as they wore their long hair, black jeans, and leather sandals.

Sean waved at his friends, then headed for the geekoid table. The intellectual elite of the school huddled in the uncoolest spot in the caf, next to the trash buckets and dirty dish line. Olivia glanced up when Sean sat down, then stuck her nose back in her book.

"Did you see the new guy working the lunch line?" Sean said. "That's Tagg, the long-distance traveler I was telling you about."

"I should have known!" Olivia said, slapping her palm against her forehead. "An alien comes to Earth to seek the pinnacle of human culture. Where else would he go but a middle school cafeteria?"

"He needs to make some money," Sean said.

"Give me a break, Winger."

"After lunch, I'll introduce you," he said. "I don't want to do it now because I don't want him to get fired."

"Of course not. An illegal alien isn't eligible for unemployment."

"You'll see," Sean promised. "But first, I want to check something. Do you have the eyepiece for your telescope?"

"What kind of nerd do you think I am, carrying around telescope parts in my bag?" Olivia said.

Sean put his hand out. Olivia sighed, then pulled out the eyepiece. He took it to the window. The sky was overcast and gray—another gloomy March day. But as he looked through the lens, the stars shone brighter than daylight.

"Look," Sean said, passing Olivia the eyepiece. "It's just like last night."

She looked. "It's still there, even in daylight! But what the heck are we looking at?"

"The Inter-Dimensional Wheel," he said.

Olivia kept her eye pressed to the lens. "Now you're a science fiction writer? You're versatile, Winger."

"It's not a story. It's how people travel in space," Sean explained. "Except they don't travel in space. They fold through dimensions. The reason we can see the Wheel is because I made the eyepiece from glass that had folded through all different dimensions. So in a weird way, it's still linked to out there, even though it's here. I mean, there. I mean, it's kind of here-and-now and there-and-then."

Olivia laughed again. "Shoddy physics, Winger. You really need to pay more attention in science." She sat back down and opened her book. Then she ate her grape nut pudding as if she didn't care whether Sean was in the here-and-now, the there-and-then, or the never-ever-after.

After lunch, Sean followed Olivia out of the cafeteria. If Mrs. Confrancisco wasn't looking, he might even be able to take her into the kitchen and introduce her to Tagg.

As he caught up to her, Olivia bumped into a fat man with a hairy face. "Excuse me," she said.

"No problem." The guy's voice rumbled like a diesel engine. The skin under his huge eyes looked like wilted lettuce.

He gave Sean the creeps. "Olivia, come on. I want to introduce you to my friend."

"Give it up," Olivia snapped. "I don't give a fig about your imaginary Tagg Orion."

Sean glanced at the dishwashing line, where Tagg was scraping dishes.

"Tagg Orion!" the big man thundered. "You son of a

Loapher! I'm going to tear off your sweat-swilling, vomit-chunking head!"

The cafeteria went dead silent. Everyone stared at the loud man with the now-purple face.

"Nice to see you again, Dinn Tauro. Sorry I can't stay and chat." Tagg snapped his scraper, catapulting a lump of acorn squash across the lunchroom.

Splat! The guy called Dinn Tauro took it in the chops.

"Why, you—" Dinn grabbed a dish of pudding and whipped it back at Tagg. At the peak of the pudding's flight, the captain of the football team stood up to get a better look at the ruckus. He took a load of butterscotch in the face.

"What the—" the football star sputtered. He grabbed a pepperoni pizza and saucered it at Dinn.

"Food fight!" someone yelled, and the air filled with meat loaf, bananas, and garlic bread. Sean hit the floor and took Olivia down with him.

"Tagg?" she whispered. "He's really real? And he's from . . . out there?"

"I tried to tell you!" Sean shoved Olivia under a table. Overhead, apples flew, ketchup spurted, and soft drinks sprayed.

"So who is this Dinn Tauro?"

"No clue," he answered. "But I intend to find out."

They crawled from table to table, through the kids who

were smart enough to take cover. Meanwhile, the morons who thought a ripping good time was worth a week of detention kept the food flying.

The football team's front line cornered Dinn Tauro and pelted him with Jell-O and ketchup. He roared like a crazed bear, whipping them with mashed potatoes and gravy.

Teachers tried to restore order. The lunch ladies ran into the lunchroom, waving spoons and towels as if they could catch the mess in midair and serve it again tomorrow.

Sean and Olivia found Tagg in the storeroom, cowering behind institutional-size cans of string beans. "Where's my ship? You've got to hide it," he cried. Then he noticed Olivia standing there, her mouth open. "Oh, hello there," Tagg said with a cozy smile.

"Heh . . ." Olivia breathed. "Heh . . . heh . . ." She couldn't even say hello.

Sean pulled the bottle out of his backpack and shoved it at Tagg. "You hide it."

Tagg threw up his hands. "I can't take that!"

"And I certainly can't take it," Squeeto said.

"Who said that?" Olivia cried.

"Two hands on my ship!" Tagg yelled.

"That's a ship?" Olivia said. Her eyes flickered between Tagg, the speck that was Squeeto, and the bottle.

"You want two hands, go see your friend Dinn Tauro,"

Sean said. "He's out there, under the mozzarella."

"You can't turn me over to that hothead," Tagg begged. "Please, Sean Winger. You have to help me."

"You said you weren't in any trouble! Now take your ship and get lost."

"I can't." Tagg moaned. He slid to the floor and hid his face in his hands.

"Yes, you can." Sean shoved the bottle at him again.

"No, he can't," Olivia said, coming out of her haze.

"He can't what?" Sean asked.

"He can't take his ship."

"Why not?"

"If what you were trying to tell me is true"—her eyes were still far away, as if she were working a mental calculator—"then to us, this is a bottle. Because we're in this dimension. But your friend Tagg's reality is the inside of the ship. How big is it inside?"

"It's huge," Sean said. "Like one of those superstores where you can buy tartar sauce, hip boots, and a fishing boat under the same roof."

"Then Tagg couldn't possibly lift the bottle," Olivia said. "We need to do it for him."

There was a huge crash from the lunchroom. The food flingers had run out of food and were now throwing tables and chairs. Dinn Tauro thundered like a hurricane. The finest of Squannacook Middle School's football team couldn't keep him busy for much longer.

"I can't keep this a secret any longer. We have to call the police," Sean said. "Or the army!"

"No!" shouted Tagg. "Don't send me to Area 51!"

"*No!*" bellowed Squeeto. "Don't blow me up with atomics!"

"No way!" said Olivia.

"Why not?" Sean asked.

"Don't you understand—I dreamed about this my whole life! Don't ask me to give up my aliens when I just found them."

"We can't handle some intergalactic crisis!" Sean said.

"Neither can adults. They have no imagination!" Olivia grabbed Sean's shoulders. "Please, Winger, let me keep them. Please!"

Even if Sean wanted to help Tagg, where could he hide the ship? His backpack was too obvious. The freezer was locked. The oven was too hot. Everything else was in plain sight.

The sink! It was crammed with pots, brimming with suds. Sean stuck the bottle into the water and watched it disappear under an orange grease slick.

Then he grabbed his remote with one hand and Olivia with the other, and escaped with Tagg and Squeeto into the *Bargain Hunter*.

11

I t didn't matter that what Tagg called a "smoke-sweating, rock-chewing lunatic" was after them. Squeeto took Olivia on a tour of the *Bargain Hunter* as if they were taking an afternoon stroll through an art gallery.

Sean didn't get how Olivia could discuss inter-dimensional physics when Dinn Tauro had threatened to tear off Tagg's head. He didn't get how Olivia could allow a nearly invisible alien to have a free ride on her earlobe.

And he sure didn't get how Tagg could have lied to him.

"I didn't lie. You asked if I was in any trouble and I said no. Because the truth was that I wasn't in trouble at that exact moment that you asked me." Tagg pulled a fabric box from one of the shelves and emptied his pockets into it. Markers, watches, silver rings, eyebrow hoops—every piece of pocket junk from Squannacook Middle School was now in Tagg Orion's possession.

Tagg suddenly tugged his ear. "Squeeto?"

"Sector Eight," Squeeto hollered. "I'm showing Olivia the damaged transfer circuits."

"It's so cool! I mean, it's not cool that your ship is broken but—" The joy in Olivia's voice echoed through the ship. She and Squeeto faded into a mumbled discussion of protons, mass transfers, and energy sinks.

Sean pulled the box away from Tagg. "Tell me about Dinn Tauro. Then you can have your toys back."

Tagg sighed. "Some customers are just never satisfied."

"Let me guess. You sold him a lava lamp that spit out frogs."

"What a great idea! The Wartts would love that—they've got these long, sticky tongues, you see. Like glue whips. They would—"

"Tagg Orion! Focus on the task at hand!" Sean shouted. "Dinn Tauro, remember?"

"Oh, him. What an incredible grump. Most sellers won't deal with him. Good guy that I am, I tried to help him." Tagg reached for the box.

Sean stuck it behind his back. "What did you do?"

"I scoured the outer planets until I found a Dream Ring for him," Tagg said. "The Dream Ring is designed to funnel all your dreadful dreams into the darkest dimension. I ask you, Sean Winger—is a hundred thousand galactic credits too much to ask for happiness?"

"You can't buy happiness," Sean said automatically.

"Yes, you can," Tagg said. "Indeed you can. And I'm the guy to sell it to you."

"Like you did to Dinn Tauro? If he's got this Dream Ring, then why is he so obviously ticked off?"

"There's a story going around that Dinn is having a little, wee bit of a problem with the ring." Tagg lowered his voice. "It's rumored—mind you, it's just a rumor—that the ring may be spawning dreams in the here-and-now."

"The carnival we saw! It was real but unreal. That must have been his dream!" Sean said. "So whatever Dinn Tauro dreams actually happens?"

"That's what they're saying."

"And how did he find us at school?"

"I'm guessing his sensors picked up a signal from the lens you made for Olivia Ricci. It must have some residue from the I-D Wheel. So, I guess that makes this all your fault, Sean Winger." Tagg grinned. "Don't flash that Shoftissi glass around."

"My fault?" Sean yelped. "What about you? Don't you owe the guy a refund?"

"No exchanges, returns, or refunds. That's my policy."

"But the Dream Ring is broken!"

"Dinn Tauro took that chance when he bought secondhand merchandise," Tagg said. "You know what they say."

"What?" Sean said.

86

"Let the buyer take care," Tagg said.

"You mean Let the buyer beware. That's what we say on this planet."

"Close enough."

"You know what else we say on Earth?" Sean asked.

"What?" Tagg asked.

"The customer is always right."

"Fiddlespits." Tagg grabbed the box away. As he arranged his pile of erasers, lip glosses, and breath sprays, he looked like a kid counting his Christmas presents.

Let the buyer beware. But while Dinn Tauro and Tagg Orion fought over whether the customer was always right or the buyer had to take care, what would all of this cost Sean?

Had Sean screwed up, maybe for his whole planet, by promising to hide Tagg Orion?

Franklin Zarkoff used to say that the fire called to him.

"You think the fire consumes the glass," he said. "But listen, Sean. It's the glass that captures the voice of the fire and makes it speak forever."

Glass is a living thing, always in motion. Like the rippled panes of an old house, glass moves in its own time. Even in the fire, it still moves under its own will unless the artist's hand guides it. Then it can be blown, shaped, bent, cut, and created to be whatever the artist has dreamed.

If the artist knows what he's doing.

Frank told Sean that he had sure hands and a visionary's eye. By the time Sean was eight years old, he handled a small blowpipe with ease. By the time he was ten, he had mastered simple techniques of shaping and finishing. When he was eleven, Sean was ready to be trained in the Zarkoff techniques, known only to Franklin Zarkoff.

As Frank got sick, then sicker, Sean's glassblowing sessions grew few, then fewer. When Sean was twelve, Franklin Zarkoff died. Even so, whenever he sat in front of the furnace, Sean felt the old man was right there with him.

Too bad he was silent.

Sean had been waiting for over a year to blow glass in a furnace again. The time was here, now that he had moved the bottle and hidden it well—in Mrs. Joslyn's compost pile.

But now that the time had finally come, Sean couldn't remember when to turn, how much to blow, and where to cut.

He worked for three hours but all he made was a nasty mess. A blue sag was supposed to be a vase. A silver crumple was supposed to be a star. A crystal lump was supposed to be a paperweight.

"I can sell these!" Tagg said. "I think . . . maybe the

outer rings of . . . someplace."

Squeeto chimed in. "Didn't you tell me that art is in the eye of the beholder?"

"Of course!" Tagg said. "Why, the Muck Snorters of Klum prize belly warts."

"Absolutely," Squeeto said. "The Swagerts of GinSing capture the flatulence of the sea scourge, then hang the boil balls on their ears."

"The Lamebrains of Igle make sculptures out of nasal effluent," Tagg added. "Why, once I sold an Igle masterpiece for eight thousand G.C.s. Have you considered creating art out of your body snot, Sean Winger? You could—"

"Enough!" Sean yelped.

"Tomorrow you'll do better," Tagg said weakly.

Tomorrow? There were only six tomorrows between Sean and the Hollis Art Fair.

Six days to learn what it takes a lifetime to master.

12

Sean dragged himself out of bed before sunrise on Saturday morning. A week away from the Hollis Art Fair and he still had no entry. He was working up his courage to whoosh back into the bottle for another furnace session when Olivia called.

An hour later, they met at Crane's Neck Beach. The Sun was just breaking the horizon, flooding the ocean with gold. Sean could see the glass rising out of the fire. A deep cobalt blue that he would shape into a mighty breaking wave, then crest with real gold. *Tomorrow Rising*, he would call it. He would never sell it; he would keep it for himself to remind him that, because life goes on, art must go on.

"What're you staring at?" Olivia asked.

"The very improbable," he mumbled.

"The Sun coming up is a certainty," Olivia said.

And my turning it into a pile of scrap glass is another certainty, Sean thought. Without Franklin Zarkoff to help him, he wasn't going to make anything worthy of the Hollis Art Fair. And without winning the Hollis, he didn't have a chance of going to Monadnock Museum School. Without the museum school, Sean would never rise out of this Dumpster he called his life.

"Earth to Winger! Did you bring the remote?" Olivia said.

"Yeah, but you have to be within twenty feet of the bottle to use it," he said. "And I left that at home. Hidden."

Olivia grabbed the remote out of his hand. "Not a problem."

"So what's this about?"

"Did you ever wonder why I asked you to help me on that science assignment?"

Sketching the constellations was only two days ago. But it seemed like a hundred years. "My good looks? My fancy car? Oh, I know—my stock portfolio!"

"I don't know why you insist on being such a jerk." Olivia stomped away.

"Wait! I'm sorry. I do have this tendency to act stupid under stress." He caught up to Olivia. "So why did you ask me? It obviously wasn't my grade point average."

"Think, Winger. What's the most special thing about you? The one thing you wouldn't change, even if someone offered you a hundred million dollars."

He didn't even hesitate. "My vision."

"Exactly!" Olivia said. "You're always looking somewhere

that's *not here*. Call it imagination or fantasy or a dream world—but to get to someplace spectacular you have to have the vision to believe that it exists. Which I thought you had."

"I do!" Sean cried. "You know I do!"

"Good," Olivia said. "Then you won't mind coming with me now." The rocks were wet and slippery, but Olivia scampered up them like she couldn't wait to get to the top.

Sean followed carefully. Not breaking his hands was a priority. At the top, he found Olivia under a huge boulder, crouched in a sheltered patch of sand.

"Is this where we're going?" Sean asked.

"Not exactly." Olivia grabbed his hand, then pointed the remote at what looked like a beer keg. Only, instead of being made of aluminum or wood, it was all glass.

"No, Olivia! Don't! " Sean shouted. "I think that's Dinn Tauro's ship!"

—Sean tumbled with Olivia into a mist of warmth and ease. He could have stayed there forever, melting into the cushion of oblivion, leaving behind the chaos in his mind and not caring that he was leaving behind his art—

Suddenly, the Universe crashed over them! Planets exploding, suns blazing, mountains soaring, monsters bellowing, swords flashing, birds swooping, skies falling.

Sean curled into himself, trying to stop the visual assault. Olivia shook his shoulders. "Winger, look!"

He couldn't. Even closed, his eyes throbbed with images. Vines twisting, monkeys flying, lava surging, stars swimming, snakes writhing, sand trickling, ground shaking.

"It's okay." Olivia's hands were steady on his back, pushing him up. "Look."

The Universe had righted itself. They were in a chamber with no apparent doors or windows. The walls were a sleek silver and the floor was covered with balls.

Olivia pressed a ball to her face. Images swirled inside it. "I think they're like . . . movies, I guess. We accidentally triggered them all when we came in. Try it."

Sean pressed his face to the other side and stepped into a new world! The air was hot and sticky sweet. The sky was a pale blue, hung with two mellow suns. Huge birds, brazed in golds and reds, swooped overhead.

"It's real," he said with a gasp.

"No. I bet it's some sort of recording," Olivia said. "Watch." She tipped the ball one way and the birds flew backward. Tipped the other way, the world marched forward again.

Olivia was either insane or fearless, Sean thought. Fearless, he decided. Olivia Ricci feared nothing except being left behind by the Universe. She fit perfectly into this movie of exotic worlds and strange sounds.

But it wasn't a movie. "Memories!" Sean said. "I think

all these balls hold memories. Didn't you feel like you were really there?"

"Whose memories?" Olivia asked.

"Stupid question for a smart girl," a voice boomed.

Olivia and Sean jumped, knocking the memory balls back into action. Images erupted again—firing lasers, flying fists, running feet—but the fuming bearlike man stomping through the memories was no image.

Dinn Tauro was very real, and he was very annoyed.

The bridge of Dinn Tauro's ship made the *Bargain Hunter* look like a taxicab. "Wow," said Olivia, gazing at the holograms of star systems and banks of flashing lights.

"Wow?" Sean whispered. "Are you nuts? We are so fried."

A tall female moved in on Sean and Olivia. With her hulking shoulders and snarling teeth, she reminded Sean of a grizzly bear. "Fried? You want to see fried? I'll show you fried!" Grizzly whipped a flashlight from her belt and shone it at a drinking cup. "How about I fry your head with my gut-burner?"

The cup sparked, then dissolved in white ashes.

"A laser gun," Olivia said, gasping. "Just like the movies."

"We're in deep doo-doo," Sean said. "Just like in the movies."

The assembled group made a noise like a sonic raspberry. *Laughter*, Sean thought. He who laughs last—well, that probably wouldn't be Olivia and him. "What do you want?" he asked. *Stupid question*, he thought.

"Tagg Orion," Grizzly said.

"He's gone," Olivia said with a straight face.

The crew laughed again, except for Dinn Tauro. He was now strangely silent, his eyes half shut. Grizzly's fingers danced on her laser pistol. *Just give me an excuse*, her eyes said.

The crew pressed in on the kids. A very short male with oatmeal-colored fuzz and a blob nose wore a bright star on his shirt. His eyes reminded Sean of Olivia's— they were the same dark brown and seemed to be always calculating some unseen equation.

The other female wore a starched white coat. Her back was straight, her eyes clear. Sean knew, even though he was light-years out of his experience, that she was some sort of medical type.

The last of the Tauroe was a thin male with shaggy hair and a pointed nose. His hungry eyes and his sharp teeth made him look like a junkyard dog.

"You lie! Tagg Orion is still here," the star guy said. "There's been no vessel-sized Inter-Dimensional activity on this spoke. Just the little playtimes of you Earth sprouts."

95

"Well," Olivia said in a convincing huff. "It's not like the Inter-Dimensional Wheel is the only way to travel. Are you aware of Faustian physics?"

Olivia launched into a poker-faced lecture. Within minutes, even Junkyard Dog was screaming about Heisenberg's uncertainties and Von Puken's theories of irony.

Dinn Tauro's eyes were almost closed now, his head slumped sideways. Sean saw something glittering out of his neck fuzz. Glass, crystal, and glowing—it must be the Dream Ring! How could anything so awesome cause so much trouble? But he knew too well that beauty often brings pain and conflict. His own family was proof of that.

Dinn Tauro's eyes snapped open. "Enough!" he shouted. "You both reek of Tagg Orion! That galling scent of the sweet but empty promise. It makes me want to turn my guts out."

Junkyard Dog shoved a bucket in Dinn Tauro's face. "Feel free, Your Loftiness."

Dinn Tauro growled and shoved the bucket aside. "I will not honor these butt-kissing, scamp-shielding sprouts by exposing my bile to them. Off with their heads!"

Sean wanted to scream *"Stop!"* but his tongue was twisted somewhere around his intestines.

"Stop!" Star Man yelled.

"What is it, Navigator?" Dinn Tauro asked.

"I believe these sprouts are a protected species."

"Impossible," Grizzly yelled. Her fingers twitched on her gun. "They barely qualify as intelligent."

"Nevertheless, we can't destroy these creatures without an Amalgamation Order of Extinction," Star Man continued.

"We can destroy them if they prove a direct threat to us," Grizzly snarled.

Olivia and Sean pulled into each other, trying to appear completely harmless.

"What is your pleasure, Loftiness?" Doctor Lady asked.

Dinn Tauro's eyes were closed and his head lolled forward. His only answer was a rumbling snore.

Grizzly stepped forward, lifting her hand to slap Dinn Tauro! Star Man grabbed her hand. "No. Let our commander sleep. And"—he turned to Sean and Olivia—"let these two quivering masses of protoplasm see what their soul-stealing, heart-breaking friend, Tagg Orion, has wrought on the lofty Dinn Tauro."

Moments later, they were back on Crane's Neck Beach.

"Don't move," Grizzly snarled at Scan and Olivia. Dinn Tauro's crew had thrown the kids onto the sand like cheap beach toys.

The crew laid their sleeping commander down like he was precious crystal. Doctor Lady covered Dinn Tauro with a blanket made of fluff and fuzz.

How bizarre was this? Sean thought. A Saturday morning at Crane's Neck, and they were surrounded by aliens—aliens that were in no mood for beach volleyball.

"What are you going to do with us?" Olivia demanded.

Junkyard Dog laughed. "Whatever Dinn Tauro dreams up."

13

D inn Tauro had discovered another castle to be stormed.

The walls, looming around him like mighty warriors, were cast from the bones of heroes. The roof was lofty, elevated by the hopes of the valiant. But the floor was mud, so wet and thick that Dinn Tauro could barely march through it.

What had he always urged his loyal crew? "Onward, even when onward is impossible."

Dinn Tauro knew not to look down at his mire-held feet. Instead, he looked up, searching for the light of glory. There it was, as bright as daylight and as clear as courage. The stars sang in chorus for Dinn Tauro to move onward!

But it wasn't Dinn who was moving—it was the mud! A million mud-suckers swirled around Dinn's feet, with no purpose except to keep him from going onward.

"I must move on!" Dinn bellowed. With iron will he lifted his right foot. He took a trillion mud-suckers with him, but if that was the cost of glory, so be it. Left foot, right foot. "Onward!"

Suddenly, he was free of the mire and on the stairs. A strange sensation burned in his chest. Could this be what the Universe called hope, this expectation that if he kept moving onward he would find glory?

The light was clearer than before, so bright that Dinn breathed it, so splendid that it beat through his veins. Dinn raced up the stairs, his feet lighter than air and surer than conviction.

He floated off the stairs! Higher—faster—without doubt—he felt the light blaze through his fingers. He closed his hands, about to take hold—

"You cannot fly!"

Of course he couldn't fly! How could Dinn Tauro even dare to reach for glory when the law of gravity demanded his obedience?

Dinn Tauro fell like a stone. The thrashing mud-suckers rose to swallow him. "Inward!" they screeched. "Join us in our quest for inward and under!"

"No!" Dinn Tauro flapped his arms, trying to save himself. "If I fall in a dream and land, then I die!"

A hand reached out. Dinn Tauro grabbed it, realizing too late that it was Mr. Goblie's hand. "Is your homework done, young man?"

"Noooooo!" Dinn howled. He let go, preferring mud-suckers to detention. But he landed on his feet, held up by a cold wind and battered by a relentless tide. The castle had vomited him out to this desolate place of sand and ocean and no glory that Dinn could see.

Dinn Tauro knelt on the sand and prepared his headstone. "So this is how it ends," he murmured, too weary to howl his indignation at such an ignoble destiny.

This is how it ends—in a poor sleep under a sky that was folded tight.

A castle sprung from the sands of Crane's Neck!

"This is impossible by any law of physics," Olivia said. "You can't just create something out of nothing!"

"It's not *nothing*," Sean said. "What's more powerful than a dream?"

Grizzly stuck her laser in their faces. "Silence! Watch!" she demanded.

A long staircase of skeletal hands sprung from the wall and Dinn began to climb, oblivious to the ghostly fingers plucking at his feet. And then, as if summer had stepped out of the sea, a clear light shone from above.

"Pure starlight," Olivia whispered. "I knew I'd see it someday."

"Pure creation," Sean breathed. "The beginning of all beauty."

Suddenly, Dinn was flying, his arms outstretched and

his eyes filled with light.

Sean could see the glass in the fire, a dark spire, curved to catch the light. *Hope Rising*, he would call it. He would never sell it; he would give it to Dinn Tauro to take to the stars.

"Loftiness, no! You cannot fly!" Star Man yelled.

Doctor Lady slapped her hand over his mouth. Too late! Dinn fell straight and fast. Just as it seemed Dinn would splat onto the sand, he was standing just a few feet from them.

Dinn knelt and began digging with his fingers.

"Sand castles?" Olivia asked.

"A bed," Sean said.

"A grave," Star Man said, sounding like the end of the world.

"Stop him!" Doctor Lady cried.

"Not yet," Grizzly said. "These sprouts must see what Tagg Orion has wrought on our commander!"

"Why hasn't anyone else come by?" Sean whispered to Olivia. "Someone should have seen this by now and called the police."

Olivia peered through her eyepiece, then handed it to him. "This is why." A blue ball surrounded the castle, the sand, the Tauroe, and themselves.

"Probably a reflective shield," she said. "Like the blue screens they use for special effects in the movies. They must be broadcasting an image to hide what's really here."

"Enough!" Grizzly shouted. But it wasn't Sean and Olivia she was yelling at.

Dinn's crew ran to him as he disappeared under a blanket of sand. The blanket was moving—it wasn't sand, it was snakes the size of boa constrictors! Some had clawed spines, some had flaming skin, some had tongues like leather whips. Laser fire flew and swords flashed as the crew battled to retrieve Dinn Tauro.

A two-headed snake escaped the laser assault. It slid toward Olivia and Sean, training its golden eyes on them. "Join me on my quest inward and under," it hissed.

They ran for their lives—and, Sean feared, for their very souls.

14

Sean and Olivia were faint from panic and breathless from running. So the privilege of reaming out Tagg Orion fell to Squeeto Burroe.

"Inconsiderate. Untrustworthy. Thoughtless!" Squeeto bellowed.

Tagg just stood there with a stupid smile on his face. Every once in a while he'd offer up a weak defense like "Mistakes happen" or "I did my best" or "It wasn't my fault."

Olivia slumped down into the nearest piece of junk that could pass for a chair. "What are we going to do, Winger?"

"We could take the bottle back to Crane's Neck," he snapped.

"We can't do that!" she cried.

Sean had a horrible vision of Tagg Orion being swallowed up by a snake with a jaw like a crocodile's. "No, I guess we can't. Besides, I made a deal."

"What deal?" Olivia asked.

"Um . . . nothing." Before he could stop himself, Sean glanced at the control panel.

"The I-D link?" Olivia jumped out of the chair. "Fire! You're using Tagg Orion's fire!"

"It's not Tagg's fire," Sean said. "It's our Sun. Therefore, it's our fire!"

"You made a deal with Tagg Orion? Didn't you know better?"

Sean should have—after all, Tagg had lied about being a genie. But what did he know about aliens and junk traders? And it really didn't matter anyway. He needed fire and Tagg was the only one willing to give it to him.

"Why did you do it?" Olivia asked.

He told her about Monadnock Museum School and the Hollis Art Fair. Once he started, he couldn't stop. He blabbered on about how he missed Franklin Zarkoff so much it tore through his stomach and how his father's refusal to let him make glass art tore at his mind. How he just wanted good fire and good glass and everything and everyone else could just go to the darkest dimension and stay there!

"Oh my," Olivia said.

"I'm sorry," Sean said, still breathless. "I didn't mean that last part."

"I know."

"So if we throw away the bottle, I lose my chance at

being a glassblower, probably forever. And, as big a jerk as Tagg is, I'm not sure I can live with just abandoning him."

"But if we keep the bottle," Olivia said, "then we risk our lives and maybe the lives of the whole town, because Dinn Tauro won't leave until he rips someone's head off."

"Wait a minute!" Sean said. "Didn't that Star Man say we were a protected species?"

"That's right! And remember how they lasered up the carnival? I bet the castle is gone by now, too. The Tauroe are keeping themselves secret. They don't want to go shooting up the whole planet. They just want Tagg."

"He's a major pain in the butt," Sean said. "But we can't just let them have him."

"No, we can't," Olivia said. "Let me think about this."

She went into a quiet row to do what she did best. Sean grabbed his box of Shoftissi glass and tried to do what he wanted to do best. Expecting, as usual, to just screw it all up.

Five hours later, Sean was still hard at work, making a mess and planning his career as anything but a glassblower. Top of the list was sanitation engineer—with his poor grades, it was either that or emigrating to Shoftus and pumping whatever the Shoftissi pump.

While Sean sulked, Tagg rearranged his shelves. He hummed happily, as if he hadn't set a raving lunatic loose on the planet Earth.

Olivia dug into the guts of the control panel, discussing things like *multitiered processors* and *chromide capacitors* with Squeeto. They got louder and louder until Olivia finally yelled, "We can do it!"

"Do what?" Tagg and Sean asked at the same time.

"Fix your ship," Olivia said. "Some simple electronics shorted out, which is why you can't launch onto the Wheel. We can get everything we need either from the local electronics shop or online."

"Wonderful!" Tagg beamed.

"Except . . ." Olivia said, "it'll cost. Big-time."

"How big?" Tagg asked.

"About nine hundred dollars," she said.

"Where are we going to get nine hundred dollars?" Sean groaned.

Olivia laughed. "Winger, for a kid with vision, you can be awfully dense. The answer is right here, right under your nose."

Olivia went home before supper. Sean hid the bottle back in Mrs. Joslyn's compost pile.

Olivia had a great plan for tomorrow. Good thing,

because today couldn't stink any louder than it already had. Even Olivia couldn't hide her surprise when she and Squeeto had finally turned away from their calculations and looked at Sean's work.

"Oh," she'd said. "I've never been much on art, anyway."

"And what do I know?" said Squeeto Burroe, who always knew everything.

After supper, Sean lay on his bed and stared at the ceiling. His mother came in before bedtime. "What's wrong?" she asked.

"Nothing," he lied.

She put her hand on his forehead as if she could read his thoughts by taking his temperature. "Tell me."

Tell her what? That Sean had discovered beauty in a brainiac? That he had popped an alien out of a bottle? That he had seen the Universe unfold itself in unthinkable ways, spewing out wonder and nightmares?

There were too many things to tell, so Sean told her the worst. "I'm never going to be a glassblower."

"You can be whatever you want," his mother said. "As much as Dad and I love you, it's not up to us. It's up to you to make it happen, Sean."

He rolled over so his mother couldn't see his face. "I'm never going to be good enough." He squeezed his eyes shut. After a moment, the room felt empty; his mother must have left.

A little while later, she came back in, carrying a cardboard box. "Here," she said. "I guess I can't fight the inevitable any longer."

Sean sat up and swung his feet to the floor. "What's this?"

"Your inheritance." She kissed him, put the box on his bed, and left the room.

Inside were dozens of videotapes. Each tape was labeled with an elaborate, familiar scrawl.

Zarkoff technique for Hot-cast metal inclusions
Zarkoff technique for Enamel coloring
Zarkoff technique for Slumping glass

Sean rushed to the family room, turned on the VCR, and popped in the first tape he grabbed. Then he listened and watched as Frank spoke to him from the videotape.

After a while, the fire spoke to Sean, too.

15

Tagg Orion pranced like a reindeer on Christmas Eve. "This is such an amazingly primitive planet," he said. "I never thought Earth would have flea markets!"

"Are you kidding?" Olivia huffed as she carried a box almost bigger than herself. "Every weekend, parking lots all over America are filled with people selling junk."

Tagg beamed. "You know what I always say: One jeeber's junk—"

"We know!" Sean shouted.

Olivia and Sean had persuaded Mrs. Ricci to drive them on Sunday to the Derry Flea Market, two towns over from Squannacook. Their story was that they had to research product negotiation in an open marketplace. Sean's parents agreed to pick them up later that afternoon.

Their parents had no clue that they were transporting an alien in a bottle along with their kids.

Olivia and Sean pooled their allowances to rent a

twenty-dollar space. They stashed the bottle under the Porta-Potties and whooshed in and out, loading up the table with the finest of Tagg's junk.

"Pure happiness," Sean said.

"Are you nuts?" Olivia said, unpacking another box of alien doodads. "This trash?"

"That." Sean pointed to Tagg. "That is what pure happiness looks like." Tagg's eyes were dreamy. His smile glimmered like a marquee: *Come and see! Come and buy!*

A blast of an air horn sounded the market's opening. Within seconds, people surged through the aisles, devising their browsing strategies and searching for early-bird scores.

"Let the selling begin!" Tagg sang.

"See?" Sean said. "Happy."

"Just as along as Tagg Orion's happiness doesn't turn into our misery," Olivia said.

The task was almost impossible. The danger was surely mortal. The secrecy was cruelly absolute. The reward was basically negligible. But Olivia Ricci had never been happier in her life.

Up to my elbows in an alien spacecraft, Olivia thought. *Now, this is truly happiness.*

After helping Tagg and Sean set up their tables, she

whooshed back into the bottle. She and Squeeto began preparing the burned circuits in the launch system for the new electronics. It wouldn't be long before the *Bargain Hunter* was ready to launch onto the I-D Wheel.

"You will come back?" Olivia asked. "Right, Squeeto?" Squeeto sat quietly on her earlobe. He weighed nothing, but somehow she could always tell where he was.

"I'd like to come back, Olivia Ricci," he finally said. "But you may have noticed that Tagg Orion is rather unreliable."

"Can't you get someone from Leo Minor to bring you back to Earth to visit me?"

"Leo Minor doesn't exist," Squeeto said.

"Of course it does. I've seen it every night since I was six. Except for those short seasons when it's under our horizon."

"It exists," Squeeto agreed. "Just not for me."

"You mean—you really don't want to go to Leo Minor?"

"Of course not."

"But you and Tagg—"

"We've been together for so long that we don't really remember where or how we met. Or how Leo Minor became part of our mythology."

"But Tagg doesn't look older than, say, twenty-five years," Olivia said.

"Remember, the Inter-Dimensional Wheel spins out-side time. Tagg and I never stay in one place long enough to have time catch up with us. Or to make friends."

"Except with each other," Olivia said.

"Maybe."

"If you aren't Tagg's friend," she asked, "then what are you?"

"I suppose I'm the voice in Tagg Orion's ear," Squeeto finally said. "Who knows how much trouble he'd get into without me?"

"Very true." Olivia knew Dinn Tauro was more dan-gerous than a nest of scorpions. How much worse would Tagg do without Squeeto to watch out for him?

"Squeeto," Olivia said. "Could I please see what you look like?"

Squeeto's silence was so complete that Olivia feared the Burroe had left her. Finally he said, "No one has ever asked to see me before."

"Even Tagg?"

"Especially Tagg."

"Then I would be doubly honored if you would let me see you," Olivia said.

"You'll find there's not much to me," Squeeto said.

"Don't ever say that! Small doesn't mean insignifi-cant!"

Olivia felt Squeeto settle on her fingertip. She squinted,

but the little speck never resolved past a brown blur.

"Don't move, Squeeto. Give me a minute." Olivia brought out her telescope eyepiece. "Aha! There you are."

Though impossibly tiny, Squeeto Burroe was still a humanoid—with a head, trunk, two arms, two legs. He was a shiny brown, like a coffee bean. His eyes were a dazzling purple. His teeth were square and shiny, and his grin stretched across his face.

Squeeto's trunk was covered with fuzz. Olivia didn't think it would be polite to ask him if it was fur or clothing. It wasn't until he twirled like a ballerina that she realized he had three sets of wings. The upper two were the largest, and folded into a brown sheath. His underwings were so transparent that she could barely see them.

Olivia felt like she was going to burst with the absolute wonder of the Universe. "I'm so pleased to meet you, Squeeto Burroe."

"Likewise," Squeeto said. "Now that we've been properly introduced, we should probably get back to work."

Olivia wished she could keep Squeeto with her forever. But it wouldn't do to let Tagg Orion wander the galaxies all by himself.

It wouldn't do at all.

Sean had never seen so much junk in one place. Tables brimmed with the usual flea market fare: bicycles, jewelry, furniture, clothing, lamps, skis, books, jars, dishes, games. Then there was the bizarre and nearly unmentionable: preworn underwear, nasal hair clippers, moose heads, used toilets, denture cups.

"Who buys all this stuff?" Sean asked.

"Why, intellifolks everywhere love bargains," Tagg said.

"Hey! What's this?" A sharp-eyed woman picked up a jar of green slime.

Sean groaned. How had that escaped his careful screening? He hoped that green glob was just an alien pickle or Martian fungus.

"Loapher giblets," Tagg said. "Unique for erasing skin wrinkles."

"Unique?" The woman snorted. "I've got a dozen lotions like that at home."

Sean stuck the jar under the table. He didn't know what Loaphers were, but he suspected that their giblets were disgusting, if not outright toxic.

Tagg's merchandise moved faster than hot dogs at a ball game. Sean had to whoosh into the bottle frequently to replenish their stock. After the situation with the Loapher giblets, he screened the items even more carefully. Sean labeled a stack of *National GeoGalactic* magazines as comic books. The gargantuan nose rings of Lux were relabeled as silver belts.

Sean refused to let Tagg bring out the two-headed kitten that sang "You Are My Solar Shine" in a thousand languages, including Vegan slang and Texan twang. And no way would he allow Tagg to sell snudwucker seeds. Who knew what monsters could grow from those?

Around midmorning, Tagg Orion demonstrated something he called the Circling Ball to a couple of wise-mouthed teenagers. "Go ahead, throw it," Tagg said. "It'll orbit the Earth, then come back to you."

The boy in the backward baseball cap laughed. "Bullcrap!"

"It's true. And only five bucks," Tagg said. "If you don't want it, give it to your girlfriend."

Purple Spike poked Backward Cap. "Like a dude this sketchy has a girlfriend!"

"You mean that girl over there isn't your girlfriend?" Tagg nodded at a blond cheerleader type picking through estate jewelry at a nearby table. "She's been watching you this whole time. I just assumed—" Tagg leaned closer to Backward Cap. "Of course, it could be the Circler she's interested in."

"Three bucks," Backward Cap said.

"Four. And that just covers the cost," Tagg countered.

Backward Cap kicked the dirt, then pulled out four

grubby one-dollar bills.

"Now let me show you how it works." Tagg heaved the ball into the air.

"Hey!" Backward Cap yelped. "I just paid for that."

"Not to worry," Tagg said. "It'll come back after it orbits the Earth."

"This is such bull." Purple Spike laughed.

"You don't believe me? Look!" Tagg pointed. A streak of light cut across the morning sky.

A group of squealing girls came by, wanting to buy bracelets that were really nostril expanders from the Snouts of Virgon. Sean was so busy counting out change, he forgot that Tagg's Circling Ball was orbiting the Earth—for the whole world to see.

16

Olivia and Squeeto whooshed out of the bottle at midday. Squeeto stayed at the table to supervise Tagg while Olivia and Sean hunted down grilled sausages, soda, and fried dough for lunch.

"Think they would take me with them?" Olivia asked.

"Who? Them?" Sean pointed at a gang of motorcyclists. Three tough-faced bikers lugged a flamingo-pink sofa while two others toted lime-green beanbag chairs.

"Not them, you fool. I'm talking about Squeeto. And Tagg."

Sean stopped so suddenly he almost tripped a woman loaded with toilet plungers. "Watch it," she snarled, smacking Sean with what he hoped was an unused plunger.

"Are you nuts? Her," he said, pointing to Olivia. "Not you, ma'am."

The woman toddled away, her plungers restored to order.

"I think the proper term would be *inspired*," Olivia said.

"You can't leave Earth. People would . . . miss you."

"Who?"

"Your parents," Sean said.

Olivia laughed. "I have four sisters and two brothers. No one at home would even notice me gone."

"Your friends, then."

"What friends? Everyone is either intimidated by me, wants me to do their homework, or makes fun of me."

Sean grabbed her hand. He didn't know what to do with it so he just squeezed it. "Hey. I really like you. I mean, not like a boyfriend, though if you wanted to discuss that sometime, that would be okay. You probably don't think much of me. I don't blame you, either. I'm not smart, I daydream too much, I laugh at the wrong things, I break more things than I make, I'm never going to be a productive citizen. My qualifications for friendship stink. But maybe—"

"Hey, slow down!" Olivia said. "You do qualify—big-time. But this isn't about you. It's about me, jumping to the front of the line.

"It's like this, Winger. I thought I'd have to wait through college, then astronaut training, then, if I was really political, I might just get one trip in the space shuttle. One crummy trip. But after I fix the *Bargain Hunter*, I could hop on the I-D Wheel and travel the Universe. Seeking out adventure. Exotic locations. Always folding to the next planet—"

"Stop it!" Sean yelled. "For a smart girl, you're pretty dumb."

Olivia yanked her hand away. "For a sensitive artist, you're pretty rude."

"Wait!" This time Sean held her hand gently, like an artist's tool. "Tagg Orion pretends he's rushing off to the next great bargain. But he's really just running away. Pretending he's got a better dream on the next I-D fold so he doesn't have to deal with the screwup he's made on the last one."

Olivia's voice was so quiet Sean barely heard her. "Like you? Running off to Monadnock Museum School?"

"No! Of course not," he snapped. "I'm not running away. I'm running *to* what my parents and the rest of the world seem to want to keep me from—my glassblowing."

"And it's worth running to," Olivia said. "Just like my running to the stars is worth . . . almost anything. But we can't fool ourselves, can we? I mean, when we run *to* something, aren't we leaving something behind?"

Maybe, Sean thought. And so what if he was? He had plenty of things he'd be happy to leave behind. Bad grades. His father's refusal to support his glassblowing. The hole that Frank left when he died. The frustration of not making anything right.

So what if running *to* something great looked like running *away* from something else? Sometimes running away was the smart thing to do.

And Monadnock Museum School was a whole lot closer than Tagg's next stop—assuming they ever got the alien and his bottle off the planet Earth.

Sean and Olivia were counting money, eating sausage, and peddling junk when the Circling Ball returned.

Backward Cap freaked when the ball whizzed in from the east and landed in his hands. "This is just so cool," he yelped. "Got any more?" Within seconds, Tagg was swamped with kids waving money and throwing Circlers.

"Oh, shoot!" Olivia cried. "Those balls have been on the I-D Wheel! And now they're up there, flying around for everyone to see. Including Dinn Tauro."

Sean had forgotten that Dinn Tauro had tracked them to the cafeteria after he had flashed the I-D lens at the sky. "Oh, shoot!" he yelped.

"For once, I would prefer not to." Sean and Olivia whipped around. A gruff grandmother leaned over their table, clenching ham-size fists.

"Excuse me?" Olivia said.

"No, excuse me," a second grandmother said. Her hair was hidden by a shower cap, and her mouth was slathered with lipstick. She would have looked absolutely ridiculous—if her eyes hadn't been so hungry.

"We're looking for a rare item," said another grand-mother. This one had a laser-shaped bulge under her shawl.

Sean looked around in a panic. Tagg was gone; he must have seen through the grandmother disguises and disappeared, leaving Sean and Olivia to deal with his unhappy customers.

"Um . . . what rare item?" Olivia said.

"Perhaps you've seen it," the gruff grandmother said. "A bottle, about this long. A lovely item, really. Too bad it houses a snookey-stinking, puke-snorting son-of-a-Loapher named Tagg Orion."

"Dinn Tauro!" Olivia gasped.

"If you're smart enough to recognize me under this pit-scratching, belly-squeezing disguise, then you're smart enough to turn over Tagg Orion," Dinn said.

"*She* may be a genius, but no one has ever accused *me* of being smart enough for anything," Sean said. Then he dove for the Porta-Potties.

Sean looked like a purse snatcher, with his backpack on his back and five grandmothers chasing him. He was no hero, but he couldn't let Tagg Orion get his head ripped off, even if he probably did deserve it.

The flea market seemed endless—rows of tables,

stacks of merchandise, crowds of people. Sean jumped over ski boots and ducked under racks of T-shirts. Shoppers shouted and cursed but no one was louder than Dinn Tauro. "You grief-spouting, butt-kissing human! Turn over Tagg Orion!"

The grandmothers were gaining. Two security cops, with potbellies and red faces, followed the grandmothers.

Sean ducked into the row of food carts. He crawled under the fried dough wagon and made himself as small as possible. The grandmothers and security guys skidded to a stop. They looked everywhere—except under their feet.

After five long minutes, Dinn Tauro whipped off his gray wig and kicked it high into the air. His crew followed suit. Shoppers looked up in amazement, then with delight as wigs rained out of the sky.

The best bargain is a free one!

Dinn had barely ripped his housedress off when a blue-haired matron grabbed it out of his hand. As the rest of the crew abandoned their disguises, they were swamped by shoppers.

Sean breathed a sigh of relief—until he saw Dinn reach for his sword. The Tauro wasn't abandoning the chase. He was stripping down for battle! What horrible fate had Sean brought onto these innocent shoppers? They came here to buy good stuff cheap, not to get caught in some intergalactic battle.

Sean slowly crawled out from under the fried dough cart. "Here I am," he croaked.

"Grab the sprout!" Dinn hollered.

"Not so fast." One of the security guards, a chubby fellow with a stringy mustache, stepped between Sean and the defrocked grandmothers. The guard didn't look like he could arm wrestle a real grandmother, let alone an ear-steaming, paw-clenching Tauro.

Grizzly put her snout in the guard's face. "You got something you want to say?"

"Yeah!" The security guard grabbed a big fork from the sausage vendor. "No fighting on the premises."

"You got a beef, take it outside the lot," the second security guy shouted from behind the hot dog stand.

Dinn Tauro pushed by Fork Man like he was cotton candy and grabbed Sean. "You're coming with me."

Sean was frozen to the spot. "No," he choked out.

"You dare disobey me?" Dinn yanked Sean's jacket, but Sean didn't move. Dinn grabbed him with both hands and jerked. Sean stayed planted to the ground.

The entire crew surrounded Sean. They roared with anger and pulled with all their might. His jacket ripped, but he didn't move!

Feeling faint, Sean swayed backward. He easily pulled out of their grip!

How could that be? The Tauro crew had muscles of steel but they couldn't hold on to a scrawny eighth grader?

The bottle! The Tauroe couldn't move Sean, not while he wore his backpack! To Sean, the *Bargain Hunter* was a bottle. But to anyone who had traveled the I-D Wheel, the bottle was an unimaginably heavy superstore.

Grizzly whipped out a knife and slipped it under the strap of Sean's backpack. *Slash!* It cut the strap like butter.

"I know you've got Tagg Orion in there. Make him come out!" she demanded.

"I can't make Tagg Orion do anything," Sean said.

She slid the knife under the remaining strap. Once she cut the pack off, Sean would have no defense and neither would Tagg. "Help!" he yelled at the security men.

"You heard him," Fork Man snapped at Hog Dog Guy. "Help the boy."

Hot Dog Guy munched on a foot-long wiener dripping with chili. "Sorry. I'm on break."

Grizzly tightened her grip.

"Yo! Woman! Get your dirty paws off that kid."

The interior designer bikers! They were laden with fuchsia lampshades and three of Tagg's lava lamps. Olivia peeked out from among the gang. The biggest of the bikers, a bald giant with a red beard, knocked Grizzly away from Sean. "Leave the kid alone," Red Beard snarled.

Grizzly flashed the knife in his face. Red Beard whipped the knife out of her hand so fast her eyes spun. She chest-butted Red Beard. He hip-butted her back.

A shoving match erupted. Grandmas versus motorcyclists. Guards versus vendors. Shoppers versus other shoppers. Hot dogs flew, carts overturned, people and aliens grappled.

Olivia and Sean were just about to make their escape when his father appeared. "What the heck is going on here?" he roared. They could barely hear him over the cursing and shouting.

"Guess these folks didn't take the same course in negotiation that we did," Sean said.

"Let's get out of here before we get caught up in this mess," Geoff Winger said.

For once, Sean agreed with his father.

17

Tagg Orion huddled under a pile of quilts. They smelled like the underside of an Igle's tongue, but he didn't dare show his face, even if he was suffocating.

In all of the endless galaxies, Tagg had never felt so alone and helpless. Squeeto had left him in a huff to see if Dinn Tauro and his crew had either been arrested or lasered the food court to ashes. Sean and Olivia had run away and taken the *Bargain Hunter* with them.

His precious cargo! Tagg didn't know if he'd ever see his junk again. All because Dinn Tauro was such a hothead!

What was wrong with these people? Didn't they know the rule of the Universe? *Let the buyer take care.* Dinn Tauro blamed Tagg for his troubles. Was it Tagg's fault that Dinn's own mind plagued him with dark dreams?

Sean Winger blamed Tagg for his shoddy art. He had never said so, but Tagg could see it in the wounded look in the boy's face. Was it Tagg's fault that Sean didn't know how to turn glass in the fire?

Even Squeeto blamed him, for anything and everything that went wrong in the Universe! Always nagging him to take responsibility. Was it Tagg's fault that intellifolks wanted to pay almost no money, then expected perfection?

Tagg dealt in used merchandise and wholesale happiness. Most of the time, he gave his customers astounding bargains. The system worked well as long as intellifolks agreed that it was the buyer who had to take care.

So if someone ate too much and puked snickerbootles, why should Tagg worry? If someone bought a second-hand Dream Ring, then vomited his nightmares into the here-and-now, what business was it of Tagg's?

Let the buyer take care. That was good business.

I will not care, Tagg swore silently to himself as he hid from Dinn Tauro, Sean Winger, Squeeto Burroe, and the rest of the Universe who were intent on trying to make him care.

I will not care! Tagg screamed at himself—at the tumbling in his gut, the pounding in his hearts, and the gnawing in his brain.

You can't make me care!

Geoff Winger lectured for the thirty minutes it took to drive from Derry to Squannacook. "The Derry Flea Market is five blocks wide!" he said. "And you had to hang out where the trouble was?"

"It wasn't like that, Dad," Sean protested. But, in truth, it was.

"You should have gone to a nursing home, a church, maybe even a bank, to do your school project. Get involved with masses of strangers, all looking to cut corners and get a bargain, and trouble is guaranteed," his father continued. "Sean, for once, can't you take the reasonable course? The safe way?"

When they arrived at the Ricci house, Sean walked Olivia to the door. "I'm sorry my father yelled all the way home," he whispered.

"You call that yelling?" Olivia opened the front door. "Your dad was a mere whisper compared to this." Sean could hear the rowdy bangs and occasional screams from what had to be Olivia's four sisters and two brothers.

"Besides, sometimes you have to yell to get someone's attention," Squeeto said as he jumped from Olivia to Sean.

"And sometimes all that yelling makes the guy you're yelling at refuse to listen," said Sean as he walked back to the car.

"Talking to yourself?" his father asked when Sean got into the car.

"I might as well," Sean fumed. "No one else listens to me."

"I'm listening, son. What do you want to say?"

"How could you do that?" Sean asked.

"Do what?"

"Embarrass me in front of—"

"Your girlfriend?" his father asked.

"She's not my girlfriend," Sean said. "She's my friend. And she didn't need to be lectured."

"I would disagree," his father said. "You were in the middle of a riot! Apparently, neither of you has the sense to stay out of trouble."

"We knew what we were doing."

The car turned into the driveway. Geoff Winger pressed the remote to open the garage door. "No, you didn't. And since I'm responsible for your well-being, it's my duty to tell you—and I wasn't yelling—when you've acted foolishly."

"Who cares?" Sean said as he got out of the car.

"I care," his father said.

"If you really cared, you'd just butt out of my life. I don't get why you won't just leave me alone!" As Sean stomped into the kitchen, he slammed the door on his father's words.

"I love you too much to do that, son."

Monadnock Museum School was sixty miles from Squannacook. When Sean won his scholarship, he would

130

have to live there. No way would his father drive him there every day. The only lectures Sean would hear then would be on technique, tools, and materials.

But to win his ticket out of Squannacook, he had to win the Hollis Art Fair. Sean had thought it would be so easy to create something astounding once he had good fire and good glass. But, as usual, he had been wrong.

Late Sunday afternoon, Sean whooshed with Squeeto into the bottle for another furnace session. "Tagg?" he called.

"Tagg Orion!" Squeeto bellowed.

There was a long silence. "That junk-selling, promise-breaking Tagg Orion isn't in here!" Sean said. "We risked our lives to save this bottle and he's not even here!"

"I hope he's all right," Squeeto said. "I hope he knows his way home."

"What's it to you, Squeeto?" Sean snapped. "Tagg doesn't give a fig about us. He's just a chicken runaway."

"You're right!" Squeeto yelled. "He left while you and Olivia stayed to fight."

"That's right!" said Sean. He was steaming now. "And you know what?"

"What?"

"I'm sure as heck not running away," Sean vowed. "I'm not going to give up! I'm going to keep working until I make something good enough to win the Hollis Art Fair."

But what? What could Sean make that he wouldn't screw up?

The only thing Sean had made well was the lens for Olivia's telescope. Could he do that on a larger scale? Sean laid out his tools, prepared the Shoftissi glass, and began.

Slow and steady, he could hear Frank say. *Strong hands, sure hands.* He heated and rolled, then puffed, then stretched. After he shaped a gentle curve, he gathered more glass and began all over again.

Two hours later, he had created a shallow bowl of clear glass. Simple but elegant, it was a smooth oval about ten inches across and sixteen inches long.

"Hey, that's really good! I could get good credits for that." Tagg Orion had appeared out of nowhere, making Sean almost drop the bowl.

"Where were you?" Sean snapped. "You left us alone with Dinn Tauro!"

"While you were distracting that lunatic, I took the opportunity to make myself scarce," Tagg said with a huge smile.

"Coward!" Squeeto bellowed.

"Sean Winger is not a coward!" Tagg said. "I'm sure he stood up to Dinn Tauro quite nicely."

"I'm not talking about Sean Winger," Squeeto said. "I'm talking about you!"

"Whatever," Tagg said.

"That's all you have to say?" Sean yelped. "Whatever?"

"What do you want me to say?"

"How about *I'm sorry I left you to fry alone*," Sean said.

"Or, how about telling Sean Winger *Thanks for saving my miserable skin*," Squeeto added.

"Sorry and thanks," Tagg said. "Now, will you two just shut up and get off my back?"

"With pleasure," Squeeto said.

"With pleasure," Sean repeated. He put his bowl into the annealing oven to cool. Then he whooshed out of the bottle with Squeeto.

Leaving Tagg Orion alone for the second time in endless galaxies.

18

Franklin Zarkoff used to say that real artists don't create *things*, they create *life*.

Sean thought about Dinn Tauro's Dream Ring. That glittering circle of glass somehow gave life to Dinn's dreams in the here-and-now. In a strange kind of way, wasn't that what the artist was supposed to do? Give form to dreams in the here-and-now?

Sean's crystal bowl was a well-crafted piece. But it hadn't yet found its own form. Or, as Franklin Zarkoff would say—its own voice.

It was up to Sean to make his work speak. What was it he wanted to say?

Dare to make your dream come true.

That's it! He would fill the bowl with Dream Rings! He saw them rising out of the fire—one glittering, another glowing, still another mysterious and dark.

Sean pulled out a sketch pad and colored pencils and got to work. Within minutes, he knew exactly what he wanted to do. But he wasn't sure exactly how to do it.

Frank would tell him.

After supper, Sean studied the Zarkoff technique for etching glass. This was his fifth time through the tape. He wanted to get the technique correct. Besides, he enjoyed hearing Frank's voice and seeing the excitement in his face. The cancer was still years away.

His father came into the family room, looking for his reading glasses. He stopped short when he saw Frank's face. "Who gave you this!"

Sean kept his eyes glued to the television screen. "Mom."

"She shouldn't have. I asked her not to."

"I have a right to have these! Frank left these to me."

"So he could fill your head with nonsense. He did you no favor, son."

"That's your opinion." Sean turned up the volume.

"That's my experience." His father turned off the television. The tape in the VCR kept whirring along, now silent.

Sean jumped out of his chair. "I bet you wish you could turn me off like that." He was halfway through the door when his father stopped him.

"I don't want to turn you off from your interests," his father said. "I just don't want you following in Franklin Zarkoff's footsteps."

"So you don't want me to become a great artist."

"I don't want you to become a miserable human being," his father said.

"That's bull!" Sean yelled. "Frank was a great guy!"

Geoff Winger slumped down onto the sofa. He lowered his head into his hands and tugged at his hair as if he were trying to pull thoughts out of his head. After a long moment he looked up at Sean. His eyes were sad. "It wasn't that long ago, Sean. You must remember. How empty Frank's hospital room was that last month. No friends. No family."

Of course Sean remembered. He couldn't bear seeing Frank like that—bones and gray flesh, the only fire left in his eyes. And that was fading fast. Maybe he had been alone in that hospital for all those weeks. But that's the way the old man wanted it.

"We were his friends!" Sean said.

"We were his only friends." His father put his hand on Sean's shoulder. "The others had given up on him years ago. They just got sick of lending him money."

"Always money with you," Sean mumbled.

"No. Not money. Responsibility," his father said. "Keeping your word—which Frank found impossible to do."

"And besides, Frank had family!" Sean protested. "They just lived really far away so they couldn't come."

"Three ex-wives who wouldn't speak to him. And one

son, who lives within forty miles of Squannacook."

"Well, then, his son is a jerk."

"No, he's not. Not by a long shot. Eric Zarkoff was my best friend growing up. And I can tell you, growing up in the Zarkoff house was a nightmare. Frank thought he was special; he couldn't be bothered to work a real job. Things were always tight, even food. My mother used to load Eric down with homemade bread and vegetables from our garden. My father used to pay Eric to mow our lawn. I could have done it for free, but someone had to look out for Eric. His own father wouldn't. He was too consumed with being a great artist to be a decent dad."

Sean covered his ears and squeezed, as if he could push his father's words so deep that he wouldn't have to hear them or think about them. "Why are you telling me this? What do you want from me?"

His father reached up and gently pulled Sean's hands away. "Only what's best for you."

"Dad, please. Why can't you just get it? Glassblowing. That's what's best for me."

Geoff Winger stood up and wrapped his arms around his son. "Maybe I can't stop this obsession of yours. Maybe I'm stupid even to try. But I have to make sure you pursue the rest of your life with the same passion. Because creating a family and making friends and building a life—that's an art, too. It takes as much hard work as making a piece of ornamental glass.

"And it endures a whole lot longer."

Sean couldn't sleep. He tossed and turned, staring at the ceiling. Staring out the window at the clear sky, the countless stars. He wished he could talk to Olivia but it was after midnight. No way could he talk to Tagg. The alien had proved he was no friend.

And Squeeto? Well, he wanted to help, but he said he couldn't remember having a family.

Sean's father had told an awful story about Franklin Zarkoff. Was it true? Or was his father so against Sean's art that he would say anything to make him stop?

Sean didn't know what to think. What to believe.

Real artists don't create *things*, they create *life*. Why couldn't his father understand that? His mother would say that life is all about family. And that families last generations.

But Sean knew from himself and his friends that when kids got to be—what, maybe even as young as twelve—they began taking their own path. By the time they were eighteen or twenty, people were supposed to make their own way, weren't they? If families lasted forever, then people would never move on to their own lives.

Sometimes friends were closer than family. Like Franklin Zarkoff. Whatever the truth was about Frank and his own son, Sean knew this—Frank was always patient and encouraging to him. And the old man understood and believed in what was in Sean's heart, so clearly that it was as if Sean were made of glass.

Why couldn't his own father know him as well as Frank had? Why did he and his father always have to be butting heads when they were supposed to have a meeting of minds? Families didn't endure—they limped along, tripping each other up instead of helping each other along.

Art, on the other hand, lasted for years—sometimes centuries, even millennia. Sean had seen glass objects in a book, things found in old Egyptian tombs and African excavations. Long after the artist—and his family—was gone, the art lived on.

Of course, for glass to last, the artist's technique had to be excellent. Some glass art from thirty years ago had already faded or warped or even crumpled. But that was bad art and poor form, which meant it wasn't really art at all.

Tagg Orion was like that, always running to the next flea market or salvage sale. Tagg never stayed in one place long enough to create something meaningful. Maybe that's why Tagg couldn't be a good friend. He didn't understand that you have to—

Oh, jeepers, Sean thought. He'd almost used his father's word. *Endure.*

But what good was enduring if you were miserable? He should ask Dinn Tauro that one.

What really mattered? Family. Friends. Art. The stars above, the dreams within. The next bargain. Onward to glory. Was enduring the most important thing in the Universe? Or was it enough to reach for that flash of glory, even if it slipped through your hands like sand?

How could Sean be expected to figure it out? If he couldn't understand interdimensional physics—how the Universe folded and unfolded—how could he understand how his own heart folded and unfolded?

Wasn't that what art was for? To capture in an instant that which couldn't be explained in endless nights of tossing and turning?

19

T hat Monday was the beginning of spring vacation. It was as if the Universe had conspired to give Sean the time he needed to finish his entry for the Hollis Art Fair and Olivia the time she needed to work on Tagg's ship.

Olivia was in her glory, acquiring and installing the necessary electronics to repair the *Bargain Hunter*. As she worked, she sketched and took notes. Sean knew that, by the time Olivia finished college, she would have invented her own version of inter-dimensional travel.

They worked side by side, each focused on a separate task. Squeeto stayed with them the whole time, encouraging and advising.

One by one, Sean crafted a Dream Ring for each person in his life. Olivia's was clear and shining, with an upward curve. He formed his mother's ring from a rose-colored mug, then etched it with flowers. Squeeto's was small, elegant, and shaped like a star.

Sean shaped a deep red ball for Frank and tweezed tiny fingers that looked like flames. No one could put out that fire.

He made a dark blue ring to represent his father. He blew and collapsed it so many times that it was dense and heavy, allowing very little light to pass through.

He flattened, then twisted, his own ring into what Olivia called a Mobius curve—a twisted circle whose inside flowed into the outside and back to the inside. Like his vision, Sean wanted his Dream Ring to have no beginning and no end.

Glassblowing and spaceship building—it should have been the happiest week of Sean's and Olivia's lives.

But they knew Dinn Tauro was out there—furious, exhausted, and spewing nightmares—and he wouldn't give up until he found Tagg Orion.

Tagg Orion was the other blot on their horizon. They had risked their lives for him and what had he done? Abandoned them, running and hiding while Sean and Olivia faced off against Dinn Tauro.

Tagg spent the week counting and categorizing his junk. He hummed and made jokes, as if they were all one happy crew. Olivia and Sean could barely look at him. Even Squeeto had given up nagging at him and spent most of his time with Olivia. Tagg would call for the Burroe every few minutes, then pretend he didn't care when Squeeto didn't answer.

By Wednesday afternoon, Sean had completed five Dream Rings. He arranged them in the bowl, trying to plan their final position. Somehow, the work seemed incomplete, as if he were telling only part of the story. Tagg Orion and Dinn Tauro needed rings, too!

Sean made a simple ring for Tagg, then painted it with reflective material. Hollow on the inside, the outside showed you what you most wanted to see—yourself.

Sean swirled Dinn Tauro's ring into wild ridges. It was painful to look at—just as he had intended. Even Dinn Tauro didn't deserve to have his bad dreams blown back into his own here-and-now.

Sean waited until Thursday night to tell his parents that he had entered the Hollis Art Fair.

"Oh, dear," his mother said. "I wish you had given us more notice."

So you could stop me? Sean thought. *No way.* "The fair starts Saturday morning, but I have to go there Friday afternoon to set up my exhibit. If you can't give me a ride, I can take the bus to Hollis."

Dorothy Winger looked over her reading glasses at her husband. Geoff Winger folded his paper. He stared at his hands for a long moment. Then he asked, "What time do you need to get there?"

On Friday afternoon, Geoff Winger drove Sean and

143

Olivia to the Hollis Gallery to set up Sean's entry. He didn't even ask to see what was in the three cardboard boxes Sean had so carefully loaded in the car.

"Don't you want to come in with us, Mr. Winger?" Olivia asked when they arrived. "Aren't you curious to see Sean's exhibit?"

"I'll let Sean surprise me tomorrow," he said.

Little did anyone know how big a surprise it would be.

When they returned from Hollis on Friday night, Olivia declared the *Bargain Hunter* ready to launch. But Tagg was afraid to leave. "What's to stop Dinn Tauro from shooting me off the I-D fold again?"

Olivia came up with the perfect solution—except that it required Sean to go back into the Dumpster.

Crane's Neck was still deserted, even though March had finally begun to yield to spring. The air was warm and the waves were calm. The stars were so bright they seemed about to leap out of the sky.

Sean scaled up the side of the Dumpster. "You realize this is where it began?"

"And where it will end," Olivia said.

"It had better," Sean said. "We can't hide the bottle from Dinn Tauro much longer. Are you sure that his ship isn't here on Crane's Neck anymore?"

"Absolutely. I've been checking the beach and the bluff every day. They've moved it somewhere else. And I'm sure you've noticed—the castle is gone, too."

"I hope they got all the snakes."

"Jumping Jupiter, Winger. Did you have to remind me?" Olivia danced a little jig while she swept the ground near her feet with her flashlight. "So how's it going up there?"

"They can't be too far down," Sean mumbled. It was hard to search with just one hand, but no way was he going to stop holding his nose.

Beach season didn't start officially until May first. Until then, the trash cans were locked up and people threw their trash directly into the Dumpster. Since last week's trash dive there'd been a midnight pizza party. Also, three soiled diapers had been tossed into the mix, along with someone's used motor oil, two stacks of newspapers, and a plastic bag of dog poop.

Sean's hand closed around a trash bag. He gave it a tug and was rewarded with a familiar *clink-clink*. "Got it!"

"All right! Time to send Tagg Orion on his way," Olivia said.

Good riddance to bad trash, Sean thought as he slid out of the Dumpster.

As Olivia engaged the launch circuits, Squeeto perched on her ear, watching and advising. Tagg stayed in his cargo shelves, counting roaming rocks.

"Tagg, we're ready," Olivia called.

Tagg came over to the control panel. "Are you sure that you're not about to launch me into some black hole?"

Olivia shrugged. "I did my best. What is it you always say? Let the buyer beware?"

"Let the buyer take care," Tagg said automatically.

"Okay," Olivia continued. "If this works, you'll be able to launch without the Tauroe spotting your ship. Do you have any questions?"

"No," Tagg said.

"Anything you want to say before you leave?" Sean asked.

Tagg looked at him, then at Olivia. "No."

Figures, Sean thought. *Tagg wouldn't know the word* sorry *if he tripped over it.*

"I have something to say," Squeeto squeaked.

"I know, I know. Leo Minor!" Tagg snapped.

"I'm not going," Squeeto said.

"We're going! I promised I'd get you there and I will. Someday."

"I'm not going with you to Leo Minor or anywhere else," Squeeto said. "I'm staying here on Earth with Olivia Ricci and Sean Winger."

Tagg staggered hard against the nearest cargo shelf. Sean could hear roaming rocks jumping, and the two-headed kitten launched into some garbled version of "You Are My Solar Shine."

"Why would you do something so amazingly backward?" Tagg said.

"Because they're my friends," Squeeto said.

"But I'm your friend," Tagg cried.

Squeeto was silent.

"Tell him," Tagg said to Sean and Olivia. "Haven't I always—didn't I—wouldn't I—if he really needed—"

They had nothing to add to what Squeeto had already not said.

"We'd better get going," Olivia said. "I have curfew in a few minutes. I don't want to be grounded and miss the art fair tomorrow."

She pressed three buttons on the control panel. There was a weird humming. Suddenly, Sean felt light, as if he could fly without wings.

"It's working!" Olivia said. "Okay, time to execute Plan Decoy."

Sean opened the door to the Sun and dropped in the scrap bottles and jars. In seconds, the bag was empty.

"Time to go," Olivia said. For a long minute, no one moved. They all looked at Tagg. He still had nothing to say.

"If Tagg doesn't launch soon, the decoys won't mask him," Olivia said.

Sean grabbed the remote. "Have a safe trip, Tagg."

"Squeeto?" Tagg said, his voice empty of its usual good cheer.

"What, Tagg?" Squeeto said. "Did you have something to say?"

Tagg stared at Olivia's cheek, where Squeeto now perched. "Not really," he said. "Except . . . see you around."

Sean took Olivia's hand. It was ice-cold. He squeezed it gently, then he pressed the remote. They—

—*moved through nothing, which had become everything*—

—landed on the beach. Olivia grabbed her eyepiece and scanned the sky. "Look!" she said, handing Sean the lens. "It's working!"

The I-D Wheel was sparking like a firecracker. "Are those the bottles?" he asked.

"Yes!" Squeeto said. "They'll disintegrate eventually, but for now no one will be able to tell the difference between Tagg's ship and the scrap glass."

"The *Bargain Hunter*!" Sean grabbed his backpack. The bottle—and its alien—was gone.

Suddenly, Sean's whole world seemed lighter—and emptier.

Tagg Orion danced through his ship like an Xtran in a snickerbootle shop. "I'm free," he sang. "No one chasing me, no one nagging me, no one expecting anything of me."

What next? Maybe he should wheel out to a small market like the Outer Antickers. He could sell his current junk and buy new, exotic stuff to bring into the bigger marketplaces.

He wished he'd had time to take more junk off Earth. What incredible G.C.s those oddities and antiquities would fetch! But Sean Winger had been in such a hurry to get rid of him, Tagg didn't even have a moment to shop. A shame, after all Tagg had done for the boy.

At least Dinn Tauro wouldn't be a problem for much longer. As Tagg cowered under the Porta-Potties that day in Derry, he had seen Dinn pass by. The Tauro was a shadow of his rock-chewing, smoke-sweating self. A shame, but Dinn Tauro had known the risks when he let Tagg install the Dream Ring.

If Dinn had been a nicer person, watching his dreams take place in the here-and-now could have been a wonderful experience. In fact, maybe Tagg should try to locate another Dream Ring. The sweet-spirited Larks of Birdsong no doubt had lovely dreams that Tagg could sell for hefty credits.

What an incredible, amazing concept—selling sweet dreams. "Squeeto, what do you think? Should we try it?"

Silence.

"It's a joke, right, Squeeto? That's why you won't answer." Tagg fanned his face, trying to get Squeeto to respond. "That business about staying with Olivia Ricci was a bluff. You're trying to teach me a lesson, right?"

Tagg examined his face in a magni-mirror. Where was that speck called Squeeto Burroe? The speck that had nagged and nipped him through countless folds of the Universe? The speck that was—what was Squeeto Burroe really? A pain in his ear? A companion for his travels?

A friend?

Squeeto had been with him forever. Through all those glorious trips to Shuala. That squalid trip to the Rim of the Tyre. Even on the quest for the Dream Ring, bartering lava lamps for roaming rocks, roaming rocks for galloping gold, then gold for the ring.

Squeeto was always right by Tagg's ear, telling Tagg when and how he was messing up. Is that what friends did? Drove each other nuts? Nagged the stuffing out of them? Made each other better intellifolks?

Tagg didn't know. There was no profit in thinking about things like that.

But Tagg knew this: He could search all the flea markets on all the planets in all the galaxies and he'd never be able to buy what Squeeto had given him.

For free.

20

"Hey, man, I need you to work some gum for me." Luke Chang pressed three chunks of blueberry gum into Sean's hand.

"What's the big emergency?" Sean asked.

"My soldiers lost their sabers in transport," Luke said. "I tried to rechew them, but it was too disgusting, even for me."

Sean popped in the gum. His mouth would be blue for three hours but it was his duty to support a fellow artist.

He was surrounded by fellow artists here in the Monadnock Wing of the Hollis Gallery. He had never felt less like a freak and more like a part of something grand in his life. The day had finally come—Saturday, March 24. The doors would be opening to the public in a half hour, but for now students were making last-minute adjustments to their displays.

Luke's *Notre Gum Cathedral* was amazing—bricks, arches, soldiers, peasants—all formed from brightly colored gum. Even though it stunk like a candy factory sewer, it was the coolest work in the fair.

Coolest, but not the best, Sean knew.

Susan Long had entered a pastel acrylic. A knight in glowing gold armor rode a striking pink unicorn. You almost needed sunglasses to view it.

There were eighty-nine entries in all. A collection of kiln-fired pottery bowls. Watercolors of cardinals. An oil of Mount Washington. A clay bust of a very famous basketball star. A hand-woven rug made completely of faded denim.

A girl had entered a large sculpture welded from bicycle training wheels. *Growing Round*, she called it. Another kid offered a bread dough sculpture of Godzilla fighting Mothra.

Some guy entered a pup tent painted with peace signs and psychedelic daisies. *Staking Ancient History*, he called it. The only other glass artist had entered lamp-worked beads. Very attractive, Sean had to admit, but nothing like his entry.

He hadn't screwed up this time. He would win, he just knew it. He could tell by the looks of his fellow artists. Some were envious, some admiring, some angry—but no one walked by his work without stopping to stare. Even the adult artists, who were displaying in the main exhibition hall, lingered at Sean's presentation.

Dreams Rising, he had called it. He had scored each of

his rings, then suspended them inside the lip of the bowl. Later, when the sun had set and the judges came by, Sean would reveal the final surprise.

Presentation is an art in itself, Frank had always said. With the permission of the fair director, Sean had enlisted Olivia's help to redesign his display pedestal. When the time came, his design and her technical ability would make his dreams truly rise.

The Physician held open the door of the I-D link while her crewmates shoveled.

"What is this abomination?" The Waste Officer choked. Even his experience in the foul things of the galaxies had not prepared him for dealing with this unspeakable sludge.

The Physician looked at the medical hammock, where Dinn Tauro lay sleeping. "The end," she said. "The end is near and there's nothing we can do."

The Sergeant-at-Arms yanked her commander upright and slapped him. "Dinn Tauro will not die in bed," she swore. "He will go out in glory if we have to blast this planet to the darkest dimension and back."

Her fellow crew members bobbed their heads in determination.

Dinn Tauro never opened his eyes.

Dorothy Winger cried her eyes out.

"Mom, please don't do that!" Sean said. People must think he was the biggest jerk in the world, making his mother cry.

Olivia passed her a tissue. "Are you all right, Mrs. Winger?"

"I'm fine," she said through her tears. "It's just—it's so beautiful."

"You really think so?" Sean asked. He felt suddenly dizzy, as if his feet were lifting from the floor.

"You think I'd let my mascara run in public for nothing?" his mother said, now laughing.

Olivia turned to Sean's father. "What do you think, Mr. Winger?"

Don't ask! Sean wanted to yell. They didn't need the hundredth version of the Artists Starve lecture. Or maybe his father would get onto his latest rant: *Not only do artists starve but they treat their families and friends like dirt.*

"I thought you weren't allowed to blow glass at Exploring the Arts," his father said.

"I didn't," Sean said.

"Where did you do this?"

"A kind of traveling studio came through Squannacook. They're gone now," Sean said.

"Where did you get the glass? It looks very expensive. "

"It was free. Scrap drinking glasses," Sean said, "from some sort of gas station promotion."

"So what do you think, Mr. Winger?" Olivia asked again.

Before Geoff Winger could answer, a bearded man stepped in. The man was a bit younger than Sean's father, with quick hazel eyes and a quicker smile. "The technique, the balance, even the expression are all quite good," the man said. "You've done fine work here."

He handed Sean his card, but Sean didn't need it to know who he was. Peter Woods was one of the state's leading glass artists.

A woman with a long silver braid and sparkling blue eyes walked over from the *Notre Gum Cathedral.* "Are you the artist of this?" she asked Sean as she walked around *Dreams Rising.*

He nodded, too tongue-twisted to speak. Peter Woods's card was turning to mush in his sweaty hand. Someone had called him an artist!

"I'm Rebecca Fortunato," she said. "My specialty is—"

"Freeblown opaline glass," Sean managed to mutter.

The woman's face crinkled with delight. "Well, I'm complimented that you know my work," she said. "And I'm delighted to see such promise in a young artist."

Sean nodded. If Olivia hadn't leaned against him, he

might have slumped to the ground.

"I hope you'll have some time to visit us in the main exhibit hall," Peter Woods said.

"Good luck," Rebecca Fortunato said. "Though this isn't about luck at all, is it?"

Sean shook his head, then watched as the two walked away.

"So, Mr. Winger. What do you think?" Olivia asked for the third time.

"Oh, I can't compete with those accolades," he said. "So I won't even try." He put his hand on Sean's shoulder. "Well, I promised your mother we'd go out to dinner, so we'll be back when this"—his father waved his hand around as if the hall were filled with flea market junk—"is over. So we can take you home."

"Geoff, I think Sean might like us to stay," his mother said.

"No, Sean wants you to leave," Sean snapped.

"So you can have a nice, leisurely supper!" Olivia said, smiling. She took Sean's hand and squeezed it so hard he almost yelped.

"Are you sure?" his mother asked

"Absolutely," he said. "Have a good time."

Sean was silent until his parents had left the hall. Then he muttered, "Why is my father such a jerk?"

"I don't think it's a case of being a jerk," Olivia said.

"No? Then what is his problem?"

"I think he's scared."

"Scared of what? That I'll fail?" Sean asked.

"No," Olivia said. "I think he's afraid you'll succeed."

At six P.M. the Monadnock finalists were announced and asked to present their work to the judges and guests. Sean was among the five students chosen, as was Luke Chang, the watercolorist, the bread dough artist, and the training wheels sculptor.

"Tagg doesn't know what he's missing," Squeeto whispered.

"Tagg doesn't care," said Sean.

Sean, Olivia, and Susan Long cheered as Luke described how he created the *Notre Gum Cathedral*.

"Were there any disadvantages to using gum as your building material?" one of the judges asked.

"Well, my teeth turned orange," Luke said. "And I've had a crummy cold since I started. You get the whole eighth grade chewing gum for you and it's bound to get germy."

The *Growing Round* sculptor talked about scouring flea markets to find cast-off training wheels.

"Tagg would like this one," Squeeto said.

"Only if he could sell it," Olivia said.

Sean was the third presenter. As he went to the podium, he saw his parents standing near the door. His mother smiled and waved. She must have insisted that they come back in time for the judging. His father studied his fingernails.

Sean described the different techniques he used for each of the Dream Rings. After taking a few questions from the judges, Sean stepped away from the podium and went to his sculpture.

"I'd like to complete the presentation," Sean said, then waved to Olivia. She slowly turned down the lights in the hall.

Olivia had helped him rig a spotlight under *Dreams Rising*. As the beam came on, Sean's *Dreams* filled the hall with glittering shapes and light.

Sean felt faint. Was it from the excitement? Or from everyone gasping in unison, sucking all the air out of the room?

Each Dream Ring caught the light in a different way. Frank's circle of flames burned red, while Olivia's ring seemed about to float on its own inspiration. Squeeto's star twinkled. Dorothy Winger's rose-shaded ring cast a soft light.

Tagg's sphere reflected all the light, bouncing it off the other rings and causing a shining ruckus. Dinn Tauro's ring twisted the light in a tortured path.

Geoff Winger's ring seemed to pull all the light into itself so all that remained was a dark hole.

Luke was the first one to look up. "Ohmigosh!" he yelled. The light shining through the rings cast brilliant shapes on the ceiling, so radiant that it seemed as if they would rise through the roof.

The crowd was stunned silent. Everyone stared upward, except Sean's father. As he moved through the crowd, the sparkles of *Dreams Rising* made it seem as if he were walking through the Inter-Dimensional Wheel.

"I didn't know," his father said, trying to push through the people.

"You didn't know what?" Sean asked over the heads of the judges.

Geoff Winger stopped about ten feet away. "I didn't know what was in you."

His father seemed to be waiting for him to take the next step. But Sean couldn't seem to move. His heart felt like the ring he had made for his father, pulling everything in and giving nothing back. "I tried to tell you," he finally said.

Suddenly, the lights came on. "No! We're not done looking at it!" someone yelled.

People crowded in on Sean. As he accepted congratulations, he lost sight of his father. Moments later, Olivia pushed to his side, looking like she had seen a ghost.

"What went wrong?" Sean asked. "You were supposed to give me a full two minutes before you turned the lights back on."

"That went wrong." Olivia pointed at the ceiling.

Why hadn't Sean noticed them earlier? He had been too focused on setting up the pedestal, too annoyed from fighting with his father, too worried about breaking his exhibit.

There were six skylights in the ceiling.

21

"**Y**ou just flashed the whole sky with I-D glass," Squeeto tried to whisper.

"Maybe Dinn Tauro didn't see the light show," Sean said. "Maybe he's gone."

"And maybe he's not," Olivia said. "What are we going to do?"

The crowd's attention was focused on the bread dough sculptor. He was trying to persuade the judges that Mothra and Godzilla were cultural icons. "You can't think of them as just brute monsters," he argued. "You've got to consider their passion, their integrity, their persistence. Rather than monsters, think of them as—"

"Rats!" a woman screamed.

People in the crowd weaved, hopped, and yelped.

"Maybe it's some kid's performance art?" Sean asked. Then two rats the size of cats cut between him and Olivia.

"Dinn Tauro!" Olivia said.

"He sure knows how to make an entrance," Squeeto said.

A security guard raced through the hall brandishing a broom. Following him was a gallery guide pushing a snow shovel. A minute later, the two rats had been swept out the side door.

As the crowd began to settle, Sean saw his mother motioning for him to come to her. He smiled but shook his head no. If Dinn Tauro was in this crowd, Sean didn't want to endanger his parents. Besides, no matter what, he wasn't leaving *Dreams Rising*.

The bread dough sculptor resumed his presentation. "You have to beat the dough into submission," he said. "The artist has to always be in control. The artist has to— Whoa, Mama!"

The bread dough sculptor grabbed Godzilla and flung it into a flock of huge rats. The rats mobbed Godzilla and chewed through the lacquer like buzzsaws.

Someone yanked Sean's arm—his father, yelling over the screams. "It's not safe. We've got to get out of here."

"Don't believe it!" Sean said. "It's just a bad dream!" He pulled out of his father's grasp. His father lunged for him, only to be swept back by frantic people.

Sean pushed Olivia. "Go on out," he shouted. "I'll be okay."

"No!" she said. "I started this with you. I'm not leaving."

They linked arms and stood against the crowd. By the time they pushed back to *Dreams Rising* the hall was empty—except for a horde of giant rats, now licking up the crumbs of Godzilla.

Sean lifted *Dreams Rising* off the pedestal and hugged it to his chest.

"We've got to get out of here!" Squeeto wailed.

"No! We have to find Dinn Tauro," Olivia said.

"Then what?" Squeeto cried.

"Then we'll wake him up," Sean said. "Maybe if we just tell him we're sorry, he'll go away."

"And maybe rats will fly," Squeeto muttered.

"Oh, I sincerely hope not," Olivia said.

The *Bargain Hunter* had linked to an I-D Hub in no time. Tagg let his ship spin there while he tried to decide which fold to wheel out on.

Back to Shuala? That flea market ran all day, every day. Lots of action there, plenty of G.C.s floating around.

Maybe he should go to Xtra. Those greedy Xtrans would buy anything they could shove down their food muzzlers. All that gum and candy he had traded for at Sean Winger's school would fetch a good price there.

What was Sean Winger doing now? Probably belly-aching with Squeeto Burroe and Olivia Ricci about what a jerk Tagg Orion was. *Irresponsible. Selfish. Shortsighted.* You don't call your friends dirty words like that, even if you think you're trying to keep them out of trouble.

Besides, how much trouble was Tagg really in? Everyone knew Dinn Tauro was just a gasbag. He wouldn't have really ripped off Tagg Orion's head. He just needed something to yell and scream about, that's all. That grump was always looking for attention.

What was Dinn Tauro doing now? Tagg hadn't seen Dinn's ship come out of the fold and onto the Wheel. Maybe that smoke-sweating, rock-chewing lunatic was just too tired for a fight. Maybe he was ready to give up.

Except Dinn Tauro never gave up.

What if the Tauro had decided to stay on Earth? That ridiculous Squeeto Burroe should have come with Tagg, where he belonged. After all that time Squeeto had spent with him, you would think he had learned that you can't stay anywhere too long.

So what if Dinn had decided to make his last stand on Earth? Hadn't Tagg warned Sean Winger that the buyer should take care? Why should Tagg even worry about what was happening on Earth right now?

Where was the profit in that?

The Hollis Gallery had been evacuated. Reports of rats the size of German shepherds had drawn the police, the National Guard, and the media to the gallery. The parking lot was mobbed with police cars, chattering people, and anxious artists.

A command center was set up. Eyewitnesses were interviewed. Strategies were discussed, then abandoned. No one wanted to face the rats quite yet.

Sean and Olivia huddled in the gallery's kitchen. Sean had called his mother's cell phone and told her that they had gone with some other kids to a pizza place down the road. "I hate to lie," he told Olivia and Squeeto. "But my father would never believe the truth anyway."

"You'd hate it even worse if the Amalgamation mounted a cleanup operation," Squeeto warned. "We've got to stop this madness before those cameras start broadcasting to your satellites."

"We've got to find Dinn Tauro!" Olivia said. She peeked out the door.

Outside, the rats scurried around the student exhibits, looking for something else to devour. Sean still had his arms wrapped around *Dreams Rising*. After receiving praise from artists as acclaimed as Wood and Fortunato, he couldn't bear to see anything happen to it.

"We have to make it through the rats first," Sean said. "And I think I know how."

Four large caterer's carts were lined up at the receiving door. A reception had been planned following the announcement of the Monadnock prize. The judging seemed a lifetime ago.

Leave it to me to screw up my one chance, Sean thought. Maybe Dinn Tauro was Tagg's fault—but Tagg was Sean's fault. He should have left the bottle in the ocean. But if he had done that, then the glass would still be in Sean's mind and not in *Dreams Rising.*

Sean balanced his sculpture on the top of a cart. He began pushing through the doors. Olivia followed him with a second cart.

"Just like my dream," Sean mumbled.

"Not mine!" Olivia said. "Extraterrestrial contact was supposed to be peaceful. Enlightening! Not this idiocy."

"It's like coloring outside the lines," Sean said as he tossed canapés to the ravenous rats.

"Huh?" Olivia couldn't throw melon slices fast enough. The cat-size beggars crowded around her, their snouts twitching.

"Your extraterrestrial contact—you thought you could control it. But when you color outside the lines, you might get something you don't expect," Sean continued. "Like art."

"Like life," Squeeto said.

Sean and Olivia lured the rats to a utility closet with chocolate eclairs and locked them in. Then they went looking for Dinn Tauro.

They found him asleep in the *Staking Ancient History* pup tent. The floor of the tent overflowed with a black goop that smelled like a ruptured septic tank.

"Wake him up!" Olivia cried. "Before he dreams something unstoppable, like a Tyrannosaurus Rex!"

Sean tried to shake the Tauro awake but he was as immovable as a boulder. "He won't budge!"

"He's exhausted," Olivia said. She raised her hand, flattened her palm, ready to strike. She squeezed her eyes closed and—

—Sean grabbed her hand. "No!"

"This is how his crew wakes him up!"

"We're not his crew," Sean said.

"No, you are not."

Sean whipped around to see Grizzly and the rest of the Tauroe crew moving in on them. They dragged the kids out of the tent.

"You are Dinn Tauro's enemies and Tagg Orion's friends," Grizzly growled.

"Tagg Orion is gone," Olivia said.

"You lie!" Junkyard Dog snarled.

"No, they don't," Star Man said, juggling what looked like a hand-held computer. "His vessel's profile has just been noted at an I-D Hub three galaxies away from us."

"Let's go get him," Grizzly said.

"We can't!" Doctor Lady cried. "Our commander won't last long enough to make the link-and-launch. This is where we must take our stand."

"Take your stand? What are you talking about?" Sean said. What kind of cowboy talk was that? This was an art gallery, not the Alamo. They couldn't laser this place like they had the carnival and castle. Could they?

"The mighty Dinn Tauro will not leave this life without retribution," Grizzly vowed. "Since Tagg Orion is not here, he will go to his grave with the next-best vengeance we can offer him."

Then she aimed her laser gun straight at Olivia's forehead.

22

"No!" Sean screamed.

As he jumped to push Olivia out of the way, he slammed into a brick wall. Which wasn't a brick wall at all. It was—

"Tagg Orion!" Squeeto squealed, Olivia cried, and Grizzly snarled, all together.

"At last!" Dinn Tauro rose from his sludge as if he were carrying the whole Universe on his back. His eyes drooped almost to his chin. Every few seconds they would pop wide, then collapse again. The Tauro was using his last ounce of strength to stay awake.

"Why did you come back, Tagg?" asked Squeeto.

"I was thinking . . . it seemed . . . I wondered if . . . I guess I might possibly have something I need to say," Tagg finally muttered.

Grizzly stuck her laser in Tagg's chest. "I can't wait to hear your last words."

Tagg turned to Olivia. "I'm sorry, Olivia Ricci."

"Sorry?" Olivia said. "Sorry for what?"

"I know you wanted something better from the Universe. A brave hero, a great leader, a wise teacher. Not a flea marketer."

"Well, Tagg, you might not be a dashing hero, but you sure are unique," Olivia said.

Tagg smiled broadly. "Thanks." Then he turned to Sean. "I'm sorry, Sean Winger."

"That's okay." Sean could barely speak. How much more could his world be shaken today? Accolades from glassblowers extraordinaire. Giant rats. Gut-burners. And now, somewhere out on the I-D Wheel, Tagg Orion had tripped over the word *sorry*. And he'd brought it back with him.

"No, it's not okay," Tagg said. "I lied to you when I told you I wasn't in trouble. Then I ran away when you and Olivia needed help. I might be cheap, but I shouldn't be that cheap."

"In that case, I'm sorry I fished your bottle out of the ocean," Sean said.

"Oh," Tagg said, his smile fading. "I guess I deserve that. I've really screwed up your life."

"No, you didn't! Well, yes you did," Sean said. "But if I had just left you there, then Dinn Tauro wouldn't have found you."

"I would have found him in the bottom of the deepest black hole!" Dinn roared.

"Where's Squeeto?" Tagg said.

"I'm here," Squeeto said. His dark speck moved across Olivia's cheek.

"I'm sorry," Tagg said. "I wasn't a very good friend."

"You came back," Squeeto said. "That's being a good friend."

"Only because I was so lonely," Tagg whispered.

"That's a good enough deal for me," Squeeto said. His speck moved in a flash, from Olivia to Tagg Orion's earlobe.

"Are we done with this gut-wrenching, tear-jerking reunion yet?" Dinn Tauro growled.

Sean poked Tagg. "Don't you have something you want to say to Dinn Tauro?"

"Yeah," said Tagg. "If you weren't such a rip-snorting, foul-mouthing grouch, you wouldn't have such bad dreams."

"Youch!" Tagg grabbed his ear. "I thought you were my friend, Squeeto."

"I am, Tagg Orion. But someone has to keep you in line," Squeeto said. "Now, don't you have something else to say to Dinn Tauro?"

"Dinn Tauro, I'm sorry that the Dream Ring isn't working right and I'm sorry that there's nothing I can do to make it better."

"There is one thing you can do," Dinn Tauro said.

"You can join me in my miserable demise." Dinn Tauro ripped the laser out of Grizzly's hands. With gritted teeth and popped eyes, Dinn slowly raised the weapon. An orange triangle appeared on Tagg's chest.

"No!" Sean yelled. "Killing Tagg won't help you!"

"It is the last comfort I have," Dinn Tauro said. His hand slid to the trigger.

"I expected better from you!" Olivia cried. "I expected people from the stars to be civilized and wise and peaceful."

"Let the buyer take care," Dinn said. His finger tightened.

"No!" Squeeto squealed.

Dinn's eyes fluttered, then he slumped sideways. The laser fired, blasting the *Notre Gum Cathedral* into a sticky soup.

"Run!" Tagg yelled.

Junkyard Dog slammed his weapon into Tagg's back.

"Never mind," Tagg whimpered.

Dinn Tauro yawned long and wide. Then he popped open his eyes, lifted the laser, and sighted again on Tagg Orion's chest.

"It was nice knowing you, Olivia Ricci and Sean Winger," Tagg said.

Dinn Tauro's hand moved to the trigger. His eyes were wide and his legs seemed strong, as if he were drawing strength from blasting Tagg Orion out of this world.

"We have to stop this," Sean whispered to Olivia.

"What can we do against a laser?" Olivia's eyes flooded with tears. "The power of amplified light may be the most tremendous force in the known Universe."

Sean's heart pounded. There was something more powerful than light!

As Dinn Tauro's finger tightened, Sean reached for *Dreams Rising*.

Whomp! There was a burst of white light just as Sean stuck his glass sculpture in front of Tagg's chest.

Dreams Rising grabbed the laser light and sent it dancing everywhere. Colors exploded like pulsars, throbbing and coursing across the walls, ceiling, and floor.

The Tauroe crew dived for cover. Tagg Orion fainted. Olivia slumped to the floor, crying with relief. Sean stood and cheered as rings of light flooded the hall.

As if he were a statue, Dinn Tauro kept his finger on the trigger. Sean kept his glass bowl between the laser beam and Tagg Orion.

Art versus rage, Sean thought as he tried to keep his knees from wobbling. *Beauty versus pain. Creation versus frustration, exhaustion, disappointment, and brute power.*

There's nothing more powerful than a dream.

To take his mind off the increasing heat in the glass, Sean watched his dreams painting laser light all over the hall. Rose petals from his mother's ring spread over the floor. Squeeto's star sparkled bright and high on the ceiling. Olivia's ring spun the light in a clear circle, like a halo of glory. Tagg's ring deflected the laser, zinging little bursts all around the gallery, igniting Mothra.

Dinn Tauro's ring twisted the light so it writhed in painful squiggles.

The bowl was now glowing. Sean's hands were screaming with pain. Dinn's laser began to fade. *It must be losing power*, Sean thought. Would it run out before he was forced to drop the glass?

What did it matter anyway? If he outlasted Dinn Tauro's laser, the crew had a shipload of others. He'd really screwed up big-time, thinking he could go against alien warriors. Why not just give up? *Get a job, be a productive citizen, forget my dreams—* "No!" Sean yelled. He tipped the bowl so that the laser beam caught his father's ring.

It drank in the light. Geoff Winger's Dream Ring held the light and took the heat.

Finally, Dinn Tauro dropped the laser. "Even this ends in nothing," he said wearily.

Sean carefully put *Dreams Rising* back on its pedestal.

"Tagg, get up!" Olivia said, pushing at Tagg with her foot.

"Get up!" Squeeto bellowed.

Tagg slowly dragged himself off the floor. As they

helped him up, Sean saw Dinn Tauro slumping against Doctor Lady.

Grizzly grabbed Junkyard Dog's weapon. "Nice light show," she said. "But I'm not as careful as my commander. I don't care who gets in my way."

She raised her laser gun. Her hand moved to the trigger.

"Stop!" an authoritative voice commanded. Sean turned to see his father striding into the hall. Grizzly turned her laser on Geoff Winger.

"Dad, no!" Sean cried. "Go away!"

"Not without you, son." His father stepped up to Grizzly. "I don't know who you are or what your problem is, but put that gun down this instant."

Grizzly laughed as she tightened her finger on the trigger. "Gun? My stupid Earth savage, this is a gutburner."

Crack.

"What's that?" Olivia cried.

Crack. The sound that every glassblower fears. The sound of glass about to—

"Hit the floor!" Sean yelled.

Tagg, Olivia, Geoff Winger, and Sean dived for the floor just as—

Pop!

Dreams Rising exploded into a thousand pieces.

23

Sean didn't know his father had it in him.

Geoff Winger listened to the story of an alien in a bottle almost without blinking. A fine line of perspiration broke out over his eyebrows, but other than that, Geoff Winger took the introduction of the extraterrestrials with an almost unearthly calm.

"I'll deal with you later about taking in strangers," he said to Sean. "Now, what seems to be the problem among these people?"

"Intellifolks," the Doctor Lady muttered.

"What?" Geoff Winger asked.

"*Intellifolks* is the galactic word for *people*," Olivia explained. Then she launched into an explanation of the Dream Ring.

Geoff Winger widened his eyes at her tales of castles and carnivals. When Olivia showed him the odious slime in the pup tent and the horde of rats locked up in the utility closet, he said, "Okay, I get it."

"And you can't take this Dream Ring back?" Mr.

Winger asked Tagg.

"No returns, no exchanges. Besides . . ." Tagg's voice trailed off into a mumble.

"What did you say?"

"That the only way to get it off is to take my head off!" Dinn Tauro bellowed.

"It's hardwired into His Loftiness's brain," Doctor lady explained.

"That could be a problem," Geoff Winger said. "Has anyone tried to fix it?"

"Um . . . no," said Tagg.

The Tauroe crew all shook their heads and beat their chests.

Sean shrugged.

"Why didn't I think of that?" Olivia cried.

"Okay, let's take a look." Mr. Winger reached for Dinn Tauro's neck. Grizzly almost tore his hands off.

"Didn't I tell you to sit down?" Geoff Winger snapped.

She sat so fast her knees cracked.

Dinn Tauro tipped his neck every which way while Geoff Winger ran his fingers over the ring. "Why, I think this is glass," he said. "Sean, check this out."

Sean touched the ring, trying not to make unauthorized contact with Dinn Tauro. There were just so many times Grizzly could be made to sit.

"There's a crack," Sean said. "A hairline fissure."

"You'll have to fix it," his father said.

"Me? Why me?"

"You're the glassblower."

"It's just a hobby," Sean said.

"That's not what you've been telling me for five years."

"I'm not good enough!" Sean cried.

"You have to be!" Dinn Tauro commanded.

"Dad! Tell them! I'll screw it up!"

"No, you won't," his father said. "For the sake of this poor man—I mean, this poor intellifolk—and the rest of us, you can't fail."

Things went from bizarre to unbelievable. Geoff Winger retrieved his wife from the gallery's parking lot while Sean hid the *Bargain Hunter* in his backpack and shoved the pack into the caterer's cart.

Meanwhile, the Star Man set up the blue bubble and displayed an image of a million rats scampering around the perimeter of the gallery. "That should keep us from being disturbed," he said.

Then they all whooshed—

—*through that splendid nothing that led to everything, the velvet promise of a Universe unfolding*—

—into the bottle.

Dorothy Winger was sheet white. "This is so unbelievable," she said.

"Where's your imagination?" her husband said. His

body was loose and his manner confident, but Sean noticed that his father's whole body shook slightly, as if the floor were trembling under his feet.

While Sean melted the best of his Shoftissi glass, Tagg took the Wingers and the Tauroe on a tour of his cargo shelves. Dinn Tauro slumped onto the floor and fell into such a deep sleep Sean couldn't tell if he was even breathing.

Until the first sugarplum appeared in midair.

Every sprout loves snickerbootles. Little Dinn was no different—though raised by his mothers and fathers on roots and rocks, he longed for sweets and delights.

Little Dinn had been put in his pen to recharge his muscles and restore his vigor. He had been commanded to sleep, not to dream.

But dreams tickled at him, laughing and singing their way into existence. And why not? He wasn't springing boulder-rollers or gutter rats from his slumber. Dinn Tauro was hatching snickerbootles.

Sweeter than birdsong, lighter than spring air, more pleasing than victory, more delicate than a hard-won peace—snickerbootles were rarer than happiness.

Little Dinn wouldn't let happiness slip away again. He lifted into the air, swooping like a flutterfly through the snickerbootles. Breathing in sweetness and sugar and bliss.

Then it started to rain.

"No!" he howled.

The snickerbootles melted into green slime. The slime took quick root and crawled up the walls of Dinn's world. Grasping fingers shredded Dinn's flutters. Without his hope to carry him, he fell to the planet Earth.

Hungry mouths smacked scummy kisses at him. "Join us in our quest for inward and under!"

"Never!" shouted Dinn. He struggled to get up, but strong hands held him in place.

"Don't move, Mr. Tauro," a bird warbled.

"We're trying to help you," a rock said.

"Inward and under," the slime sputtered. "Sleep forever in my haze."

"Hold on, Loftiness!" the very air commanded.

"I can't," Dinn cried. "I'm just too tired . . ."

It was bad enough when candy began appearing in the air, but when the rain started, Sean was spooked.

When the walls and floor of the *Bargain Hunter* became smacking mouths, burping out sewer breath, Sean wanted to whoosh out of the bottle forever. Even the Dumpster would be better than this!

The Doctor Lady and Sean's father held Dinn Tauro

while Sean readied the glass patch. Sean's mother stroked the Tauro's hand and whispered encouragement. The Tauro was being pulled down by some unseen but powerful force. All their combined strength and encouragement would soon not be enough to hold him.

"Hurry!" the Doctor Lady yelled.

Sean used his smallest blowpipe to catch a tiny glob of glass. His hand shook so much that the glass flew off, narrowly missing his mother.

"Relax. You can do it," she whispered.

"I can't," Sean said.

"You must," his father said.

"Now you're ordering me to be a glassblower?" Sean said, trying to joke. "Aren't you afraid I'll starve?"

"I'd rather these scum-suckers on the walls do the starving," Geoff Winger said with a weak laugh. "They're looking for a good meal and I'd prefer it not be us."

Olivia put her hand over Sean's. "You made dreams rise, Winger," she said. "You can put them back in their place."

"I don't think I can," Sean said, trying to gather more glass. Olivia held his forearm steady. Then he felt his father's hands on his shoulders. The Navigator had taken Mr. Winger's place holding down Dinn Tauro.

"All we're asking is that you do your best," Sean's father said.

182

"When you said you didn't know what I had in me," Sean said. "What did you mean?"

"I knew you had the vision," his father said. "I just didn't know you had the self-discipline and determination to make it happen. But now I do. So use that famous vision of yours, son. See this happen, then make it happen."

Sean looked past the tortured face of Dinn Tauro, the confusion on Tagg's face, the frantic speck that was Squeeto. He let his mind and heart wander through the scum-sucking, slime-spewing walls of the *Bargain Hunter* into the darkness that robbed Dinn Tauro's mind and soul of their rest—

—and he saw the glass rising from the fire.

Pure. Sparkling. Waiting for someone to breathe it to life.

You were given those hands as a gift, Franklin Zarkoff had said. *Follow them into the chaos and pull out beauty.*

Sean saw it as clearly as he saw his mother's face shining with hope. He saw it as clearly as the stars in Olivia's eyes and the courage in Dinn Tauro's heart. *Life Rising*, he would call it. He would never sell it; it wasn't his to sell.

And he would never give it away because it wasn't his to give.

It was only his to share.

He dipped the blowpipe into the glass. With a quick

183

flick, he twisted the gather to secure it. Then he opened the door to the Sun and let the fire of the Universe call the glass to life.

When the glass was ready to be formed, he put the blowpipe to his mouth and puffed. With a quick roll on the marvering table, he flattened the tiny bubble into a long oval.

Then he held his breath and laid the hot glass over the crack in the Dream Ring on Dinn Tauro's neck.

24

The Hollis Gallery was closed for a week for fumigation. No rats were ever recovered. Rumors that people were finding them in their septic tanks, swimming pools, and toilets were never confirmed.

The Monadnock prize could not be awarded because half of the finalists' exhibits had been destroyed. *Dreams Rising* was assumed to have been shattered by the crowd as it surged to escape the rats. *Godzilla and Mothra* was rightly thought to have been eaten by the rats. No one was quite sure what had happened to Luke's *Notre Gum Cathedral*; it had melted into a gummy mess. *Staking Ancient History*, while not a finalist, was nevertheless declared to be a biohazard and had to be destroyed.

The judges distributed letters to the student artists. They expressed their regrets and promised to waive the entry fee for next year's fair.

Sean crumpled the letter and trashed it. Next year was too late for him.

Asleep under his fuzzer, Dinn Tauro slept through the next solar cycle. There was no way to tell if his dreams were sweet because he kept them to himself.

Dorothy Winger invited Olivia to spend all day Sunday with them. "We're going on a field trip," Mrs. Winger told Mrs. Ricci. Mrs. Ricci, busy with her other six kids, never asked where they were going.

The Navigator took Mrs. Winger, Olivia, Squeeto, and Sean on a quick trip to the Big Dipper, where they made a whirlwind tour of four planets and one asteroid belt. On a planet lush with orange grass and spiky trees, they released a gutter rat the size of an elephant.

"Sweet dreams," the Navigator called as the creature lumbered through a meadow of purple flowers.

The trip was like nothing Olivia had ever imagined or Sean had dreamed. Though it took them two months in Inter-Dimensional time, they were back before supper.

Their last stop was the Earth's moon. Navigator parked *The Eliminator* on the dark side so they could all watch the planet rise over the horizon.

Dorothy Winger cried. Olivia held her breath, afraid to exhale because it might all disappear.

Sean had a sudden vision of a rich green world under a sparkling blue sky. It would take two blowpipes; nesting glass within glass was an advanced technique. He could do it, he knew he could.

He just didn't know who was going to teach him. But he couldn't worry about that—there was no profit in worrying. He just had to believe it would somehow happen.

Home Rising, he would call it. He would never sell it and he would never give it away.

He would keep it to remind himself that dreams do come true.

Mr. Winger declined to go with them on their galactic tour. "There's only so far my imagination will stretch in one weekend," he said with a sigh. "Maybe next time."

Besides, someone had to take Tagg shopping. He had three hundred and sixteen dollars left over from the flea market. Geoff Winger took Tagg to All-Mart, where you could buy anything from frozen peas to denture cream to swimming pools.

Tagg thought he had reached the joyous end of the Universe. "What's this place called again?" he asked Mr. Winger.

"A superstore," Mr. Winger said.

"Why don't we have these in the Amalgamation?" Tagg said. "We are so primitive."

Geoff Winger laughed. "If we have time, we'll stop at the mall." When he explained what a mall was, Tagg grabbed his chest. He wasn't sure that his two hearts could take so much excitement in one solar cycle.

While some traveled the galaxy and others traveled Squannacook, Grizzly and Junkyard Dog shopped from Tagg's cargo shelves. Grizzly wept real tears when the two-headed kitten sang "You Are My Solar Shine" in Tauroe.

Junkyard Dog ate the Loapher giblets and was giddy for the rest of the day.

Dinn Tauro woke up in time for supper. It was a warm spring night. The group clustered on the Wingers' deck for a farewell cookout. Mr. Winger grilled hot dogs and hamburgers while Dinn sat in a lounge chair and sipped lemonade. He was almost smiling.

"What next?" asked Mrs. Winger.

"We're off to Eruptus," the Navigator said. "There's a fire-breathing, intellifolk-eating gargolyte that needs some tending to."

"And Dinn Tauro is the guy to do it!" Dinn bellowed. Then he took another sip of his lemonade, and almost smiled again.

"What about you, Tagg?" Olivia asked.

Tagg glanced at Geoff Winger. Mr. Winger cleared his throat. "Tagg is going to be staying here for a while."

"Here?" Dorothy Winger gasped, looking at her house.

"Not exactly here," her husband said. "He will be lodging at Mrs. Joslyn's. The dear lady has wanted someone to help clean out her attic and cellar and garage for years. And Tagg will also be gainfully employed."

"Where?" Sean asked. "Not back at the school cafeteria, I hope."

"All-Mart!" Tagg said. "I'm their new assistant manager. When I get the hang of this retail thing, Squeeto and I will head out to open the first mall ever in the Amalgamated Planets!"

Sean and Olivia steered Mr. Winger off the deck so they could have a private word with him. "Dad, are you sure you want Tagg to stay here on Earth?" Sean asked.

"Why not?" his father said. "He's a nice enough guy. A little optimistic for my taste, but it's different people—intellifolks—that make the world interesting. Besides, what harm can he do?"

Olivia groaned and looked at Sean.

"Just use your imagination, Dad." Sean sighed. "The sky is the limit!"

25

It was a putrid way to end what had been an unbelievably wonderful week—sitting at the kitchen table, trying to figure out which high school to register for. The form was due tomorrow, and Sean was miserably trying to map out his future.

What was the use if he couldn't do what he was meant to? Sean would have won the Hollis prize if they hadn't cancelled the judging! He had seen it in the eyes of the judges, his fellow artists, the guests at the gallery.

He had even seen it in his father's eyes. "You deserve to go to Monadnock Museum School," his father had said last night. "But it costs as much as a private college. Even if I got a second job—"

"It's okay, Dad," Sean had said. "It's up to me to make my own life happen anyway." The disappointment tore at his gut but he tried to put it behind him. There was no profit in crying over spilled snickerbootles.

But which school to choose? He'd love to go to the exam school with Olivia, but no way he'd get in. Luke

Chang was going there, too, but Luke had always managed to snag good marks between gum chewing and cathedral building.

Sean was stuck with the high school, the charter school, or the tech school. Appropriate for everyone except for an aspiring master glassblower.

He was trying to figure out how to flip a coin three ways when the doorbell rang. He didn't think much about it until his parents came into the kitchen with Peter Woods.

Sean jumped up, almost knocking over his chair. "H-hi," he stammered.

Peter Woods extended his hand. Sean shook it. "Good hands," Mr. Woods said. "Strong. Agile. The hands of a craftsman."

"I wish," Sean said.

"That's why I'm here," Mr. Woods said.

Sean looked at his parents, confused. His mother smiled, his father shrugged.

"We saw a lot of promising student art at the Hollis Art Fair," Mr. Woods said. "And we realized that very few kids are in a position to attend a school like Monadnock. So Rebecca Fortunato and I have decided to start an art program for public high school students. And we're not talking just oils and clay—we're talking rigorous disciplines."

"Like glassblowing?" Sean said, almost afraid to breathe.

"Definitely glassblowing," Mr. Woods said. "Artists all over the state will donate one or two afternoons a week to apprentice students in their studios. By the way, I hope you'll agree to work with me, Sean."

"Yes!" Sean's heart pounded so hard he thought it would shake the house. "Dad, is it okay?"

"I don't see why not," his father said.

"There's only one issue," Mr. Woods said.

"What?" Sean yelped. "I'll do anything!"

"An apprentice program will require at least two after-noons away from school," he continued. "We're talking six-to-eight-hour blocks of time to make this work. Our apprentices need to be in a flexible academic program that will allow them studio time."

"And the only school that offers a flexible schedule—" Dorothy Winger began.

"—is the exam school," Sean said. He sank into his chair and lowered his head onto the table. There was no way in a thousand galaxies he would ever qualify.

"You can qualify," his father said, as if he had read Sean's mind. "You've got three months to improve your grades and retake the entrance exam. It'll take a lot of hard work but I know you can do it."

"Dad, I stink at school." Sean moaned.

"So, you're just going to give up? Just like that?" his

father said. "You didn't let me stop you from glassblowing. Are you going to stop yourself from going to the best school for you?"

"No," Sean mumbled.

"What?" his father snapped. "I can't hear you!"

"I said *NO*!" Sean yelled. "Where do I start? How do I start?"

"You're not too far behind in your humanities courses. Start by catching up on your English and history homework," his mother said. "And giving it your best, not just doing it to say you've done it."

"I can do that!" Sean said. "But what about science and math? I can't figure out those subjects by myself."

"So you get help," his father said. "And I know just the person for the job."

"Earth to Winger!" Olivia said, punching Sean on the arm. "What is the value of x?"

"Forty-two," he said. His mind might be on algebra but his eyes were on the horizon.

The wind coming off the water at Crane's Neck was crisp and salty. The sand under them was still warm from the Sun even though it had set an hour earlier. There was still an edge to the air; when spring comes to Squannacook, the ocean is always the last to surrender.

Sean turned off the flashlight and closed his notebook.

He and Olivia looked up together. The night was a work of art. Countless stars. Measureless sky. Perfect light in perfect darkness.

"Did you ever wish on one?" Sean said.

"Just one? Try all of them." Olivia laughed. "Every night since I was six years old."

"And . . ."

"It came true," Olivia said. "Not exactly how I imagined it would be, but—somehow it was more amazing than I ever dreamed."

"So now what? Do we stop wishing?"

"Not in a thousand galaxies," Olivia said with a grin.

"And that will be just the beginning," Sean agreed.